KISS OF A STAR

ARTEMIS LUPINE SERIES, BOOK TWO

CATHERINE BANKS

TURBO KITTEN
INDUSTRIES

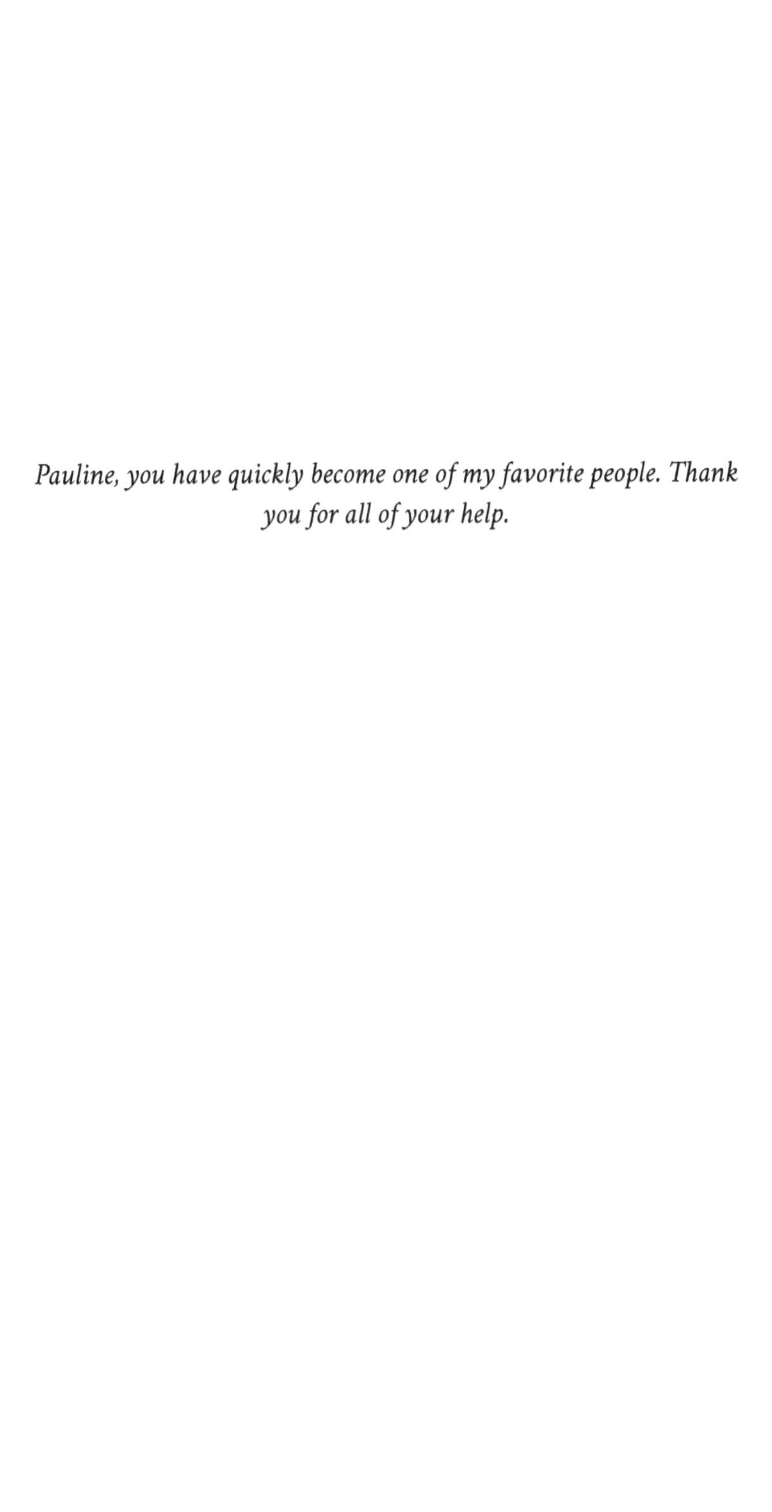

Pauline, you have quickly become one of my favorite people. Thank you for all of your help.

Special thanks to the following people
who backed my Kickstarter and helped
these gorgeous books out into the world.

Amanda Jenkins
Anij Fallows
Arlene Medder
Brandy Robinson
Ceciley Snook
D. T. Brook
Davide B.
Deissy Hermunslie
Emily Suzanne Davis
Emjrabbitwolf
Fawn of the Woods
Francesco Tehrani
Gary Phillips
Helen Jensen
Jamie Forster
Jeff Lewis
Jennifer & Jamie Wallace
Jennifer Laslie
Jon Tarbox
Ken Anderson
Kylie Corley

Louise Kendall
Matthea W. Ross
MelX
Michelle Fritz
Michelle Johnson
Michelle R. McFarlin
R.J. Blain
Ran Frimark
Russell Nohelty
Russell Ventimeglia
Stormie Harlan
Synergica
Taka Angevine
Tara Harrington
Zack Newcomb
Amanda Haynes
Erin Hayes
Amber
Emma
The Creative Fund
Rebecca Laffar-Smith

ONE

A res, Koda, Matt, and I left France early in the morning, but without Victor or Jean Pierre. They were forced to stay behind to discuss some impending threat, which I assumed was regarding the attacks on the other countries. The connection between Ares and me was stronger than ever. I needed to have constant physical contact. We grabbed the first flight, and I felt my worry ease as we left France.

"Where are we going, Ares?" I asked as I relaxed against the seat.

Ares smiled happily. "My home, in Germany."

My eyes widened for a minute and I then smiled. He did have German features, as did Koda and Matt.

My smile left as a thought came to mind. "Great. Big, German, werewolf women. You couldn't have come from a country with small women, could you?"

Ares kissed my cheek. "You'll be fine."

I smiled evilly. "Maybe I'll just toast them with a fireball."

Ares shook his head. "You aren't allowed to use your Sidhe

powers unless absolutely necessary. No one must know that you have them."

I groaned. "Great. I finally get powers and now I can't use them." After a little accident, this morning, where I'd torched a hand towel, we realized I was able to use my Sidhe powers.

The plane touched down, and we walked through the airport to the waiting vehicle. A man, standing at least seven feet tall, leaned against the hood of a strange European vehicle. He smiled at Ares and bowed at the waist. "Greetings, Ares."

Ares bowed. "Greetings, Brother."

The man turned to me and smiled as he spoke to Ares. "I see your taste in women has improved."

My lip twitched in a snarl, and Ares wrapped his arm around my shoulders. "This is my mate, Ulger, and your Princess."

Ulger dropped to one knee in front of me. "Forgive me, Princess. I had not heard that Prince Ares took a mate."

I looked at Ares for help, but he just smiled. "Uh, you're forgiven," I said awkwardly.

Ulger stood and kissed the back of my hand. "Thank you, Princess."

Ares cleared his throat, and Ulger turned to him. "Darius wanted me to tell you that Darren has escaped our trackers. We aren't sure where he has gone, but we've sent additional trackers to pick up his trail."

"My dad got away? He's still alive?" My voice grew higher in pitch.

Ares wrapped his arm around my shoulders and whispered, "I won't let him hurt you."

His words and touch calmed my nerves, and I relaxed against his side. "I know."

Ares opened the back door of the car and smiled brightly. "Are you ready to meet more of our kind?"

I huffed. "No, but what choice do I have?"

We drove in silence for a few hours, and my mind began wandering. What were these women like? Were they all as beautiful as the ones I had seen? Ares tried to pull me into his lap, and I resisted, pulling away from him. He frowned. "What's wrong?"

I saw the look of concern on his face and forced the words out before I lost my nerve. "If I let you, would you leave me, for these women?"

Ares smiled, his blue eyes sparkling. "Not a chance. Artemis. I love you. I thought you were over this?"

"I'm sorry. I'm just nervous." I leaned against him and closed my eyes.

He whispered, "You are the only woman for me. Whether you feel the same for me or not, I will always love you."

I looked up at him and saw the pain in his eyes. He thought I was trying to tell him that I didn't truly care for him. I whispered, "I do love you, Ares."

Ares whispered, "It's our destiny to be together. Are you rehashing old issues because you don't want to discuss the new ones with me?"

"I don't know what you're talking about," I said indignantly and looked out the window to my left.

Ares whispered, "I know it's hard to deal with the fact that you aren't a virgin anymore, but isn't it satisfying to know that you'll be with the one that you gave it to, the rest of your life? Not many humans can say that."

I turned to him and kissed his lips. "I love you Ares. I'm just insecure."

He nuzzled my neck. "You have no reason to be insecure. I only have eyes for you."

Koda groaned and turned around from the passenger seat. "That was so cliché, Ares. You're how old and you couldn't come up with something better than that? I mean, you did work with Shakespeare!"

Ares frowned. "I was trying to be cute. Thank you for ruining our moment."

Koda winked at me. "Just here to help."

We drove for hours through a thick forest on an unmarked dirt road, until finally coming to a small gate with two male guards. Ulger rolled down his window and spoke in German to the guards. The guards opened the gate, bowing to our vehicle as we drove past. The trees began thinning, and we came to a large wooden barn. Ulger stopped the car, and we all climbed out. I stretched my arms up over my head, squealing as I moved.

Ares wrapped his arms around my waist and kissed my cheek. "You keep doing things like that and we won't make it to the village."

I blushed and tried to step out of his arms. "Ares, don't tease me."

He licked my cheek, holding on tightly to me. "I believe I was just saying that to you."

Ulger parked the car inside the barn and then returned to us, cracking his neck from side to side. "Ready?"

Ares nodded, smiling wide.

I asked, "Ready for what?"

Koda pulled his shirt and pants off, and then dropped to his hands and knees, shifting forms flawlessly in seconds. His wolf form was more beautiful than I remembered. I fought the urge to run my hands through his fur and turned towards Ares, who was taking his shirt off.

I sighed. "Fine, but I'm not changing back until we're somewhere I can get dressed. I don't want to parade around naked."

I took my shirt off slowly, noticing Ares watching me, and folded it nicely on the ground. I slowly pulled my pants off, wriggling my butt excessively.

Ares took a step towards me, and Koda stepped between us, whining and barking.

I stripped my underwear off quickly and changed shapes. It felt good to be a wolf again. My wolf felt ecstatic at being let out and we stretched from head to tail.

Ares sniffed my shoulder and I wagged my tail. *Let's run!*

Koda's tongue lolled out the side of his mouth. *Loser has to run around the house naked?*

Matt snorted. *No one wants to see you run around naked, anymore than we already have to.*

Ares whined. *Loser has to give the winner a back rub!*

We all ran down the dirt road, kicking up dust behind us. My muscles stretched and my blood pumped harder as I ran. The boys were lengths ahead of me when a familiar scent tickled my nose. I jumped into the forest to my right and ran through the trees towards the smell. Mom.

I could hear Ares, Koda, and Matt barking for me, but they could wait. I had to find my mom.

Ares spoke through my head. *Where are you going? What's wrong?*

I ran faster trying to follow the scent before it disappeared. *My mom's here. I can smell her.*

I jumped over a fallen log and the forest quieted. I strained my ears to listen to Ares' approaching barks, but not even the wind whispered through my ears. I changed back to human and crossed my arms over my chest. "Hello?"

A bright light darted through the trees, coming towards me. I lifted my arm to cover my eyes and the light dimmed.

A man with pale skin and blue vines etched in his arms and across his chest walked towards me. He wore only a pair of pants and was sleeker muscled than Ares, built more like a runner or swimmer.

I swallowed in fear. "Who are you?"

He spoke and the leaves rustled. "I am Achilles."

"What are you?" I asked in the silence.

"I'm Sidhe." The leaves rustled again as he spoke making me shiver involuntarily.

"What do you want? Why are you here?" I asked, growing more and more nervous and wishing Ares was here.

He smiled and held out his hand, his body glowing slightly as though a light was turned on inside of him. "I'm here for you. I'm your fiancée and I'm here to take you," he said in a soothing voice.

Ares touched my shoulder and the sounds of the forest crashed into my ears deafening me. I dropped to the ground covering my ears with my hands and moaning in pain. Ares voice boomed like thunder, "You're not taking her anywhere!"

TWO

My ears still rang as I knelt on the ground beside Ares. Koda and Matt finally found us and moved to stand behind Ares in protective stances.

"What are you doing here, Sidhe?" Ares asked between clenched teeth. I'd never seen him so mad before. His hands were balled into fists at his sides as he glared at Achilles.

Achilles glanced from Ares to me. "What is this?"

My ears finally stopped ringing, so I stood up, slightly behind Ares, and placed my hand on his shoulder. The skin to skin contact allowed some of his power to seep in and heal the damage to my ears. "It's alright, Ares. He hasn't hurt me," I said softly.

Ares' fists loosened and he grabbed one of my hands in his. I could feel his anger and worry as if they were my own. Koda whispered, "Ares."

Ares looked at my face and exhaled. The anger and worry disappeared, allowing me to breathe. *When had I stopped breathing?*

"I'm sorry," Ares said softly to me.

I kissed his cheek. "It's alright."

Achilles began glowing again and he clenched his teeth as he said, "Do not touch him."

I glared at Achilles. "I don't know who you are, but I'm not in the mood. State your business."

Achilles' eyes widened in shock for a moment, but he quickly recovered. "Artemis, I'd appreciate it if you would step away from Ares."

Ares growled. "Not going to happen. State your business."

Achilles stopped glowing and rubbed his temples, looking weary. "Of all of the werewolves in the world, why did it have to be you protecting her?"

I looked Achilles over while he was babbling and felt a smile tug up the corner of my lips. He was incredibly handsome, very close in competition for most handsome with Ares. Achilles' blue vines were beautiful and throbbed like veins. His face looked familiar, but I couldn't remember where…

Achilles spoke, interrupting my thoughts. "Artemis, I've come for you. You're mine."

I looked at him and then at Ares. "There's a lot of that going around lately. Why do you think I am yours?"

He smiled making my knees wobbly. "You're my fiancée. You were betrothed to me at birth."

I shook my head. "I can't be your fiancée. I already have a mate."

Achilles glared at Ares. "Mate? She's your mate?!"

Ares smirked. "She's my *passt genau*."

Achilles shook his head. "You're lying. You just don't want to give her to me."

Ares snarled and his anger returned. "She's my match, Achilles. She's my *mate*. She's *MINE!*"

Why was he so easily upset by this Sidhe?

Achilles narrowed his eyes. "I will not give her up simply because she's your match! I was promised the first of her mother's children. I've waited *seven hundred years* for her and I will *not* just let you have her."

Ares rubbed his face, and his anger dissipated just as quickly as it had come. "I don't want to start a war between us, but if neither of us is willing to give her up, what do you suggest we do?"

"I do not have any suggestions as of yet, but we may be able to come up with something," Achilles said softly.

Ares looked at me. "Do you have any ideas?"

I laughed loudly. "Me? I just met this guy, the first of my mother's kind, and he tells me I'm his fiancée, but how can that be since I'm already yours? He says he won't give me up, yet he doesn't have me. What do you want me to say? Kill him? No, we can't do that because for some reason that would start a war. Give me to him? Hell no! No offense, Achilles, but I love Ares and my pack. I'm not going anywhere. So, I have no ideas."

Matt spoke for the first time, making me jump. "Maybe you could cut her in half, like that story of the children fighting over the doll?"

Ares growled at Matt, who raised his hands in the air and took a step back with his head lowered submissively. "I was just kidding."

Ares closed his eyes and took a deep breath to calm himself. "Artemis, don't worry. Achilles is the Prince of the Sidhe, so a war won't start, unless we tried to kill him, which we won't. Let's get to the village and we'll discuss it more there."

Matt growled and asked, "How do we know he's telling the truth?"

Achilles looked insulted. "I'm not a *pixie*, and I wouldn't lie about this. Besides, I didn't know she was Ares' match or mate."

I held up my hands. "Stop. Can we please just get to the village? I'm hungry."

Achilles nodded. "Alright. How far is it? Should I fly?"

I gasped. "You can fly?!"

He frowned and looked at me as though I'd asked what a nose was. "Of course I can fly. You should be able to as well. Though, I suppose it depends on how strong your wolf is."

He was looking over my body, which made me realize that I was naked. A blush rushed to my cheeks instantaneously. "Enough talk. Let's go," I said as I tried to hide my embarrassment.

Achilles laughed. "She blushes? How endearing."

Ares, Koda, and Matt started running towards the village, leaving me and Achilles to catch up with them. Achilles ran beside me, watching me closely. I tried to ignore his stare, but my body began itching. I turned to him and was about to ask what his problem was when a tree appeared in front of me. I tried to stop, but couldn't slow down. At the last second, I dodged to the right.

"The trees are very interested in you," Achilles said from beside me.

"What do you mean?"

"The trees are alive, Artemis. That one that you almost hit was determined to get closer to you. I have not seen one do that in quite a while."

I groaned. "Great, now trees are out to get me. Why does my life have to be so strange? A few days ago, I was just another teenage human going to school and worrying about boys. Now I'm a half-werewolf, half-fairy, Sidhe, thing that is the mate of the Prince of the Werewolves and engaged or whatever to the Prince of the Sidhe. And *now* trees have decided they find me interesting. I would ask if it could get weirder, but I'm betting so."

We reached a clearing, and Ares growled at us in his wolf form. I dropped to my hands and knees and changed forms, rushing over to him and rubbing my head against his chest.

Don't let him touch you. Ares whispered through my mind.

Matt and Koda, also in their wolf forms, came to stand beside us. Darius, King of the Werewolves and the most frightening man I've ever met, walked towards us from around the side of a nearby house. The presence of him rose my hackles and made me back up underneath Ares until my head was below his chest and his body completely hid mine from sight.

Ares cocked his head to the side and looked at me questioningly, but Darius spoke, making him look away from me. "What is *he* doing here?" The hate was evident in Darius' voice as well as his defensive posture.

Ares looked at Darius intently for a moment and then Darius snarled. "You should have told me that he was coming with you."

Ares' body was completely still as he looked at Darius. I realized after a moment that he was communicating with Darius telepathically.

"Fine. Come meet with me in an hour," Darius said angrily before walking away from us.

You can come out now. Ares said to me.

I crawled out from under him and sat on my haunches. *He scares me.*

Ares sat beside me. *You don't have to be scared of him. He wouldn't dare hurt you now that you're my mate.*

Now? I asked in shock.

Achilles spoke softly, "Could you please stop communicating in wolf form? It's rude."

Matt growled softly at Achilles, his lips pulled back in a threatening snarl. Ares grunted, and Matt stopped, but I could still see the hate in Matt's eyes as he stared at Achilles. Ares nodded once and started walking. I followed close to Ares' side as we made our way through the town of log cabins. Men and women looked at us from the porches and from windows. Koda stayed close by my other side, scanning the houses as we passed them. Matt walked behind us with Achilles behind him.

We continued down the dirt road and past shops selling clothes and food. A small group of children stood outside one shop with ice cream cones. I stopped and stared at the cluster of toddlers and elementary-aged kids. *Children?* I mean, I knew they had children. I'd seen the ones at the first werewolf village I'd been to, but so many young ones, just walking around?

Did Ares want children? Would he want me to have a child? A werewolf child?

Artemis?

I looked at Ares and shook my head. *Nothing.*

He looked towards the kids and lifted his lips in a wolfish grin. *Yes, we do have children here, just like at the other village.*

I moved away from him. *Can we just get to wherever it is that we're going? I want to change.*

Ares shut his mouth and looked upset, his tail tight against his body. *Alright.*

He led the way in silence as we passed more houses and

more people. I couldn't believe there were so many were-wolves in one place. If the humans knew about this, it would be chaos. Of course, with the preternaturals taking over the world, the humans already had plenty of chaos to deal with. Ares finally stopped at a two-story log cabin with a wrap-around porch on both floors. It was beautiful, warm and inviting.

Ares changed forms and signaled for me to do the same. Koda and Matt changed forms and walked into the house without looking back at me. Achilles stepped onto the porch and spoke to Ares over his shoulder, "I'll wait inside."

Ares watched him walk inside with a fierce look on his face. He turned to me and his face softened. "Come on, Artemis."

I closed my eyes and pictured my human body. My body rippled, and I stood up in my human form. It still amazed me how easy it was to switch between forms. It also made me wish that I'd known about it sooner.

"Welcome to Lyngvi," Ares said.

"Lyngvi?"

Ares nodded. "That's the name of this town."

He picked me up in his arms and started walking up the stairs. "Ares!" I gasped.

He smiled and stopped in front of the door. "I want to carry you over the threshold."

"We're not married." The words left my mouth before I thought of the repercussions.

Ares' smile vanished and he looked at my face with pain pinching the corner of his eyes. "Artemis, you're my mate. That means we're married. How many times do we have to go over this?"

I had to fix the pain I'd caused him. I took a minute to plan out what to say before starting. "I'm sorry. I didn't mean it like that. I just meant that taking me over the threshold is only done when humans get married."

"This is my house, well ours now. You accepted my last name, 'Lupine', like a human married couple would have. Why can't you accept this?"

"Alright. You win. Take me into *our* house," I said quietly.

He kissed my cheek and smiled victoriously. "I always win."

He stepped over the threshold and then ran up the stairs, to the right and into a bedroom. He set me down on my feet slowly just inside the door. A large bed with luscious purple silk sheets took up most of the bedroom. A door across the room led to the bathroom with his and her sinks. A second door to the left led into a walk-in closet. The room was so welcoming and warm, that I instantly felt safe. I walked to the bed and ran my hand along the sheets. "It's beautiful."

He was still standing in the doorway, but was smiling, the full smile he so rarely wore. "I had the sheets sent from Paris specifically for you."

He started to walk into the bedroom when someone called from downstairs, "Ares."

Ares sighed loudly. "He's going to be a pest."

I walked quickly to him, feeling his irritation. "Ares, I love you and…"

Ares shook his head and kissed my lips, stopping me from continuing. "Don't worry, Artemis. It'll be fine." He rested his hand against my face and gave me his full smile again. "You're so beautiful."

A blush covered my cheeks, which made him laugh. He kissed my cheek and then yelled, "Koda!"

Koda bounded up the stairs, taking them two at a time. He

stopped at the door. "You rang?"

Ares stepped away from me slowly and stared at Koda. "You've been reassigned."

Koda's eyes widened and his voice rose a few notches higher. "What? You're reassigning me! What did I do?"

Ares placed a hand on Koda's shoulder and smiled reassuringly. "Brother, calm down. I'm reassigning you to be Artemis' guard."

Koda exhaled and put a hand against his chest. "Oh, thank the Mother. I thought you were kicking me out of the pack!"

Ares shook his head. "I couldn't kick you out of the pack. Besides, I trust only a few with her. Guard her while I speak to Achilles."

Ares kissed my cheek one more time and then walked quickly down the stairs. I watched his naked backside as he took the stairs. Koda cleared this throat. "Earth to Artemis."

I blushed again. "Sorry, Koda."

He walked into the bedroom and hopped up onto the bed. "They're going to be talking for a while."

"Why does Ares hate Achilles so much?" I asked as I sat down next to Koda on the bed.

Koda leaned back against the pillows and headboard. "That is a long story that Ares is better to tell you. I'm not trying to hide anything from you, but there's a lot to the story that I don't know."

"Is he bad?"

Koda laughed. "Bad? Well, it depends…he's not evil, if that's what you mean."

"What do you think they're going to decide?" I asked as I leaned back against the pillows next to Koda. His closeness was comforting, his scent, a mix of wolf and forest, was relaxing.

"I don't know," Koda said honestly. Koda stood up off of the bed and walked through the door that led into the closet. "You seem to be adjusting quickly," Koda said from inside the closet.

I looked down at my naked body and shrugged. "It just seems natural. I mean, I'm not going to walk around town naked or anything, but you, Matt and Ares are going to be seeing me naked a lot and, well, I just feel different now. It's like the connection with Ares has made me more mature in some ways. I'm not saying I'm completely mature, but in some aspects, I think I am. I don't know, you probably think I'm being ridiculous."

Koda walked out of the closet and tossed me a fluffy white robe. "I don't think you're being ridiculous. I think you're right. It may be your connection, or it may just be Ares."

I raised an eyebrow at him as I slipped the soft robe on. "Ares?"

"An alpha male has an intense effect on those of his pack. The alpha who cares for you after your first change, shapes you. Ares is a supreme being. He's kind, loyal, sympathetic and good. Sure, he can be intense, angry and scary at times, but overall he's smart and level-headed and very mature."

Ares stepped into the bedroom, wearing a pair of pants. "You flatter me."

Koda rolled his eyes. "I wasn't saying it for your sake."

Ares leaned against the bed post with his arms crossed. "We're still at a stalemate. I'm not sure what we're going to decide."

I crawled across the bed to sit beside where he was standing. "It's alright."

He smiled and kissed my cheek. "I've got to go speak with the king. Promise to stay away from Achilles?"

I nodded. "I'll stay here in the room with Koda."

Ares looked at Koda. "Don't let him near her and don't let anything happen to her while I'm gone."

Koda bowed at the waist. "Of course."

Ares rolled his eyes at Koda then kissed my lips. "Before I go, I want to show you something." He took my hand and I hopped down from the bed to follow.

He led me into the walk-in closet and I gaped at the size of it. I'd thought it would be a normal closet, but the room was as big as the living room at Darren's house. He led me past rows of pants, shirts and suits for men and to a back section that was recently added on. I knew it had been added on because there was still sawdust on the floor from the cabinets being put in.

Ares opened the doors to the cabinets, revealing rows of dresses, shirts, pants, undergarments and shoes. "Whose are these?" I asked in shock as I touched a soft white dress that stood out among the others.

"It's all yours," he said softly.

I turned to face him. "Mine? What do you mean mine?"

"When I started dreaming about you, I called here and had this area built for you. Then, when we were in Paris, I called again with your size and had these clothes and other items placed here." He looked at the dress I was still touching. "I bought that for you in Paris."

I smiled. "You're full of wonderful surprises, Ares. Thank you."

He took my hand. "There's more." He led me out of the closet, past Koda and to the bathroom. The bathroom was painted and decorated in a warm blue tone. The his-and-her sinks each had a toothbrush and holder next to them. Ares opened the cabinet doors under the sinks and pointed in. I looked inside and gasped. It was stocked full of feminine products, hair care products, hair brushes, curling irons, and devices I couldn't name or even imagine how to use. "I wanted you to have everything you needed. I want this to be your home as much as it is mine."

I wrapped my arms around his neck and hugged him tightly. "Thank you. You have no idea how much this means to me."

I kissed him and he rubbed his thumb down my cheek. "Why are you crying?"

I laughed and wiped at my eyes. "Sorry, it's not you. I just…with Darren I never felt loved. Sure, he provided all of the necessary items for me and he kept me safe, but it was never a loving home. It wasn't really even a home to me. But with you…I feel loved and this feels like home to me already."

Ares kissed both of my eyes softly, stopping the tears. "I'm sorry your childhood was hard. I promise that I'll do every-thing in my power to keep you safe and happy. I love you, Sunshine."

I smirked. "Sunshine?" He'd been trying to come up with a nickname for me, but I'd rejected "baby" and a few others I simply refused to let him call me.

Ares frowned. "You don't like it?"

"Why Sunshine?" I asked as I played with his hair.

"Because you gave me sunlight in my darkest day. I thought I was going crazy before I met you. Now, even with all that is happening, every time I look at you, I feel happy and warm. So, yes, 'Sunshine' is your name."

I kissed his lips quickly. "I like it."

Matt cleared his throat. "Darius isn't going to like you being late."

Ares sighed. "Duty calls."

I kissed his cheek before walking out of the bathroom and towards the closet. "I promise Koda and I will stay in the room, away from Achilles, until you get back."

Ares stopped at the bedroom door and turned back to me. "After I return, we'll be going to dinner. The whole town will be there. Will you wear the white dress?"

I saw the hopeful look on his face and curtsied, bowing my head. "Of course, my Prince."

All three men laughed. Ares rushed over and kissed my lips hard, making my heart race. "Don't forget your necklace."

I touched the diamond heart necklace which was on my upper chest. It had been a present from Ares, a sign so that everyone would know that I had his heart alone. "I've still got it on."

Ares smiled happily. "Good. I should be back in an hour or two."

I hurried into the closet and to my cabinets. I'd never had so many clothes before. I took down the white dress and stroked the soft fabric. It had spaghetti straps, a v-cut neckline and an hour glass shape like I had. I hung it on a hook on the wall and stared at the assortment of shoes. "Koda," I called softly.

He walked silently into the closet. If I hadn't been watching for him, I never would have known he was coming. "Yes?"

I pointed to the cabinet. "I need you to help me figure out what to wear with this dress."

He smiled. "No problem." He stopped in front of the cabinet and whistled. "Wow, he went all out for you. Not that I suspected he wouldn't, but this is amazing."

"I know. I'm in awe," I said dreamily.

He looked at the white dress and then at me. "Hm...alright,

here's what we're going to do." He took out a pair of white two inch heels and set them on the ground, underneath the dress. "Those." He started riffling through the underwear and I stared in shock at the thongs and lingerie in the pile. I'd never worn lingerie before. He picked up a white silk thong and set it on a chair that I hadn't noticed was next to the dress. "This." He turned to me now and frowned. "You're too big busted to go braless."

I frowned. "Thanks."

He shrugged. "Just being honest." He turned back to the cabinet and pulled out a white strapless bra. "Perfect."

I stared at the completed outfit and smiled. "You're good."

He smiled wide. "I know. Now go take a shower before you put all of that white stuff on. You've got dirt all over your legs."

I rolled my eyes. "Yes, father."

He smacked my arm playfully. "You want to look great for Ares, right?"

"Right." I gingerly took off the diamond necklace and handed it to him. "Keep it safe while I'm in the shower."

He took the necklace slowly and held it in one palm. "I promise. Now hurry. I want to tell you some things before we go to dinner."

I jogged to the bathroom and took off the robe. I started to reach for the door to shut it, but knew if Koda was supposed to be protecting me that he'd want it open. Plus, I felt safer having it open. The tub to the left of me was giant, big enough to fit all four of us in comfortably. "Koda, is this a spa or tub?" I asked curiously.

He laughed. "It's a spa."

"Why is there a spa in the bathroom?"

"Don't ask me. Ares designed this house," Koda said loudly.

The shower had no door, consisting of one long tiled wall with a shower head, which came out of the middle with a large drain in the middle of the floor. If I had been morea modest I would be running to shut the bathroom door now. I turned the shower head on and quickly scrubbed my hair and body. The shampoo and soap didn't have a smell, which was surprisingly refreshing to my nose. I hadn't realized how much the scented soaps bothered me until then. After drying off, brushing my teeth and blow drying my hair I finally felt clean. Clean for the first time in weeks. I strolled across the bedroom. "It's great to be clean."

Koda grunted. "Sure, rub it in."

My foot hit the floor awkwardly as I tried to stop in midstep before turning to him. "What?"

He sniffed his arm. "I stink, but until Ares comes back I can't shower."

"Sure, you can. I'll just do my hair and makeup in the bathroom so that you'll be protecting me while you get clean," I said with a smile.

His eyes widened. "You'd be willing to do that?"

"It's not that big of a deal. Let me put on my underwear and dress." A patch of sun was shining on the dress as I walked in. It looked too perfect for me to wear, but Ares wanted it on. The underwear felt somewhat uncomfortable as I put them on, but after a minute I barely noticed them. Of course, there wasn't much fabric to notice. The bra fit well, but without straps I felt awkward. Finally, I slipped the dress on over my head and shimmied it down my body. It was snug, but not uncomfortable. After smoothing the dress down again, I walked out of the closet and twirled in a slow circle. "What do you think?"

Koda was sitting perfectly still. I couldn't even see his

chest rising or falling with breath. "Wow," he said softly. He walked slowly towards me, making me stop twirling and blush. He smiled, but his eyes looked sad. "You're beautiful, Artemis. Ares is a lucky man."

"Does Ares know that you have feelings for Artemis?" Achilles asked from the doorway, making me jump since I hadn't realized he was there.

Koda frowned. "Of course, I have feelings for her and Ares knows. She's part of my pack."

Achilles smiled and it took my breath away. He looked like a Greek god. Wait? Achilles was a hero in Greek myths, right? Was he… "Achilles?"

Achilles looked at me and his smile faltered. "Yes?"

"Are you *the* Achilles?" I asked nervously. Being around him was uncomfortable, but not in a fearful way. He made me want to relax and be near him, which wasn't normal. Even Ares didn't feel like this to me.

Achilles smiled. "That is a long discussion that you and I will be having at a later time."

Koda grumbled. "Speaking of that, I need you to go back downstairs."

Achilles frowned at him. "Ares gave you orders to keep me away from her?"

Koda nodded. "I'm sorry, but he is my alpha and his orders were clear." Achilles looked like he wanted to argue, but Koda whispered, "Please."

Achilles sighed and rubbed his temples. "You were always my favorite, Koda. What do you want me to do, Artemis?"

"I promised Ares I would stay away from you. Please leave," I said quietly.

Achilles bowed at the waist in a graceful motion that made me stare in awe at him. "As you wish," he said before turning on his heel and heading down the hallway. The tone in which he said the words made me think of Wesley from Princess Bride and made me shiver involuntarily.

Koda handed me the diamond heart necklace and whispered, "It's a good thing Achilles is a reasonable male."

I clipped the necklace in place and walked towards the bathroom. "Come on. I want to be ready by the time Ares gets here."

Koda followed me in and started undressing. I pulled out the hair straightener and the box of makeup I'd seen earlier. Koda started the shower behind me and began singing. If he hadn't been such a talented singer, I would have laughed at him, but his voice was amazing and after a moment I hummed along as he sang. My hair didn't take long to straighten, but I was having trouble deciding what makeup to use. If I used too much makeup, I would smell funny, but I needed something to spice myself up.

Koda reached around me, making me jump and squeal. He laughed. "Sorry. I figured you had heard the water turn off."

"I was focusing on the makeup and what I should use," I said as my heart calmed down.

He held up the black eyeliner that he'd grabbed. "This around the bottom of your eyes and..." He grabbed white eyeshadow and black mascara. "These. Go light, but with just these things you'll look great."

He moved away from me and started brushing his teeth in the sink next to me.

"You have a great voice," I said to him as I applied the eyeshadow.

Koda smiled with toothpaste filling his mouth. "Thank you."

I giggled at him and finished with the makeup. My purple

eyes stood out drastically with the makeup on and with the white dress below, I looked amazing. Was I conceited? "Koda? Do you think it's conceited for me to think I look amazing now?"

Koda shook his head. "No, just truthful. Sidhe women are generally beautiful anyways."

I heard the front door open and ran towards the closet. "Shoes!"

Koda followed me in and quickly got dressed in a pair of black slacks and a deep blue button up shirt. "Don't wear the shoes," he said quickly and quietly. "I forgot that we were going to dinner with the town. We don't wear shoes to events that the King and Queen are attending."

"Why not?" I asked curiously.

"Werewolves need to be able to change at any time and shoes are often destroyed in a change because it takes too long to take them off."

Ares and Matt were walking up the stairs, so I tossed the shoes back in the cabinet and adjusted my dress.

Koda whispered, "You look great. Stop worrying."

Ares spoke from the bedroom doorway. "I'm going to change before we go, Achilles. We'll be down after I'm ready."

I hid in the cubby area where my cabinets were.

Ares walked into the closet and started rummaging around in the front area. "Why are you hiding, Artemis?"

"I'm waiting until you're ready before I let you see me," I said.

Ares began speaking to Koda, "Darius wants to speed the process up. He wants it to be finished in six months."

Koda groaned. "That's crazy. I mean it's not like it can't be done, but why? Why not just let the chaos linger for a while?"

"I need to do my hair," Ares said before walking away.

Matt peeked his head around the corner making me jump since he hadn't made a noise. "Wow, you look great."

I smiled. "Thanks."

Koda cleared his throat. "Matt, shouldn't you be getting changed?"

Matt sighed and turned around. "Alright." Matt was acting different. I couldn't put my finger on what exactly it was, but something wasn't right.

Ares spoke from nearby, "Artemis? Are you ready?"

I smoothed my dress down, checked the placement of my necklace and took a deep cleansing breath. "Yes." My heart was beating faster than it should have, but I tried to keep the smile on my face to show I wasn't that worried.

Ares stood outside of the closet in a pair of black slacks and a black button up shirt. His eyes sparkled like diamonds, catching my attention. "It looks better on you than I would have imagined," he said softly.

"You look amazing, Ares." I managed to say between the backflips the butterflies were doing in my stomach.

Ares slipped his hand in mine and kissed me on the lips. "You're breathtaking."

I inhaled his scent and the butterflies disappeared. "Thank you."

Koda stepped out of the closet with his arms spread. "What about me?" Ares shook his head and I rolled my eyes at him. Koda twirled in a circle. "So?"

"You look great, Koda," I said as I tried not to laugh.

Koda frowned. "Ares is amazing and I'm only *great*? Now you've hurt my feelings."

Matt stepped out of the closet in a pair of dark blue slacks and a white button up shirt. "We better hurry or they'll eat without us."

Ares squeezed my hand. "Let's go. I can't wait for you to meet my mother."

I groaned. "Great, the mother-in-law."

Ares kissed my cheek. "She'll love you."

Koda and Matt were discussing females as we walked down the stairs, so I chose to ignore them.

Achilles stood by the front door, leaning against it. He was wearing a black suit that hugged the curves of his body.

The sight of him made me gasp, which made Ares growl, which made me blush.

Achilles frowned at Ares, but simply asked, "Are you all ready to go?"

Matt growled. "He's coming?"

Ares growled at Matt and turned to face him. "Be kind to our guest, Matthew. You forget your place and the fact that Achilles is Prince of the Sidhe."

Matt stopped growling, but his face still showed his anger. "The Sidhe's ranks have nothing to do with me."

Achilles folded his arms across his chest. "You were always the most volatile of the three, especially towards my kind."

Matt smiled. "Thank you."

"Enough," Ares barked. "Let's go."

Achilles opened the door and walked out first. Ares followed with me by his side and Matt and Koda brought up the rear. Ares stayed silent as we walked through the town.

I looked around and noticed how deserted it was. "Where is everyone?"

"They're all gathered at the dining hall," Ares said without looking at me.

"Does everyone always go to the dining hall together?" I asked.

Achilles answered before Ares could. "No, they're all gathered to see the return of the prince and to see his mate. Ares had quite a reputation with the females so I'm sure they're all dying to see who he finally chose."

"Oh. So, I'm going to have to deal with irate women? Again?" I asked quietly.

Ares pulled my hand up and kissed the back of it. "Just remember that you're the one that has my heart."

I looked down at the diamond necklace and smiled. "Right."

Achilles stopped in front of a large concrete building, the only concrete building in the entire town.

I could see the outer wall of a castle a mile or so away. "They have a castle?"

Ares nodded. "The king and queen live in the castle."

"Wow," I said just before the doors were pushed open.

Achilles stepped to the side, allowing Ares and I to walk in first. The room was filled with wooden tables and reminded me of a medieval movie I'd watched where everyone had gathered in the hall to eat, just before being slaughtered by a grotesque creature.

All eyes turned to me and the tension in the room quadrupled.

Darius stood from his seat at the front of the room. "Greetings! Everyone, please welcome back your prince, Ares, and his mate, Artemis."

Most of the crowd clapped, but at least four women glared at me. This was going to be wonderful; I could tell.

Ares walked up the center aisle with me and bowed to Darius.

I curtsied as low as I could, keeping my head down.

Ares stood up and I matched his movements. "Greetings, King Darius. It's good to be home. My pack brothers, Matt and Koda, have come with me as well, but also my guest Prince Achilles of the Sidhe." Ares smiled as he spoke, but as he said Achilles' name, his lips thinned.

Darius lifted a brow. "Greetings, Prince Achilles and welcome." Why was he suddenly so nice? Was it just because he was in front of the rest of the pack?

Ares looked around. "Where is the queen? I was hoping she would be here."

Darius opened his mouth, but a woman spoke from the farthest corner of the building. "I'm here, good prince. I'm here."

The woman walked towards Darius. She was older, she looked to be about forty, which made me wonder how old she really was. Her gray hair was braided nicely against her back and her face looked familiar. Of course! She was Ares, Koda, and Matt's mother! The Queen kissed Darius' cheek before walking towards Ares and me. Her presence made me bow my head in submission. She was definitely an alpha female.

"Ares, my son," she said just before wrapping her arms around his shoulders. I released his hand and took a step away from him to give her room.

"Hello, Mother," Ares said lovingly. "I'd like you to meet my mate."

She gasped. "So, the rumors were true! You did take a mate." She stepped towards me and then started walking around me. She stopped in front of me again. "Look at me. I will not harm you, daughter-in-law."

I looked up slowly and smiled at her.

She stared at my face for a moment before gasping and turning on Ares. "Ares! Why? How?"

Ares frowned at her. "She's my *passt genau.*"

The room filled with gasps and loud discussions. I hadn't

realized until then that while Ares and his mother were talking, no one else in the entire building had been.

Darius raised his arms and the talking stopped. The queen looked at me again. "Who are your parents?"

"Darren is my father, but I do not know my mother's name," I said softly as I tried to hide my face from her. Did she think I was ugly? Or was I just not good enough for her son?

"What do you mean you don't know who your mother is?" she demanded.

"My mother left us when I was five. I never knew her name and my father refused to speak of her to me."

"Then how did he explain your purple eyes?" she demanded. She was angry with me about something, but I hadn't done anything, had I?

Ares took my hand and pulled me so that I was standing next to him again. "That, Mother, is something that I have already discussed with King Darius. If you would like to hear her tale, I'd prefer it be done in private." He was angry, too. What had I done to upset them?

The queen smoothed down her dress and turned her head. "Very well." She walked past me to Matt and Koda. "Matthew. Koda. My sons."

Ares released my hand to wrap his arm around my waist. "She was just caught off guard by your eyes, Artemis. It's alright," he whispered.

I nodded numbly as he led me towards a table at the front of the building. Two thirds of the women in the building glared at me as I walked with Ares. It was starting out to be a wonderful night. Darius clapped his hands. "Come now, let's eat."

THREE

A res pulled me down next to him on a wooden bench and kissed my cheek. "It's alright, Sunshine."

A woman a few rows back snickered softly, but still loud enough for me to hear. "He used to call me 'Sunshine.'"

I growled softly, and Ares whispered, "They're just trying to get a rise out of you. Ignore them."

Koda and Matt sat down at a table behind us, and women instantly surrounded them. The sight of the women flirting with them set me on edge.

Achilles sat down across from me and frowned. "Why are you jealous?"

His presence made me relax and look at him. "What?"

"You're jealous of Koda and Matt, why?" he asked.

Ares looked at me curiously as I answered. "It's not jealousy. I just…I don't want to add another person to our pack yet. I just got here and I'm finally settling in. I don't want a female coming in and trying to fight me all of the time."

Ares smiled. "You don't have to worry, Artemis. Koda and Matt aren't allowed mates."

I blinked twice. "Why not?"

"We travel around a lot and as my guards, they need to be focused on me. If they both had a mate then their attention would be focused on her, instead of me."

"That's not fair," I said to him.

Ares shrugged. "They agreed to it. It's not like I just told them that's how it was and they didn't have a choice."

Men in tuxedos started walking out of a back door, carrying large trays of meat. The men set the meat on each table and then quickly retreated back to the door they had come through.

I inhaled and turned to Ares. "Humans? You have humans working for you?"

Ares nodded as he bit into a piece of steak. "They work for us, get paid well and if they want to, we'll turn them."

Ares set a large steak on my plate. I looked at it for a moment and then started eating. It was a little overcooked for my taste, but it was still delicious. I took a drink from the cup in front of me and nearly gagged. "What is this?" I asked quietly.

"It's wine," Achilles answered. "Flown here from the vampires' winery in France."

I sniffed the drink. "I can't get drunk off of this, right?"

Ares shook his head. "Not unless you drink three or more bottles."

The girls around Matt and Koda were still giggling loudly and starting to get on my nerves. "Ares, I need to use the restroom," I whispered to him. I needed to get away from the women or I'd lose the little control I had over my wolf.

He turned around to face behind him. "Koda."

Koda looked up from his plate and then quickly hurried from his table to crouch behind us. "Yes?"

"Artemis needs to use the restroom. You're her guard now, remember?" Ares said softly.

Koda winked. "Right. Come on, Sweetheart." Koda stood and started walking towards the door the humans had used. I kissed Ares cheek before following Koda towards the door. "What's wrong?" Koda asked once we were away from everyone else.

I shook my head. "Nothing."

He rolled his eyes. "I can sense your irritation and worry. If you're worried about the women, you really shouldn't—"

I interrupted him. "I don't want to talk about it right now, please."

He pushed open the door without another word. It led into a hallway, lit with torches. He pushed open the third door on our right and waved me in. "Ladies' room."

I walked inside, and he closed the door, with him on the outside. At least he thought I was capable of using the restroom alone. I pushed open the first stall door and smiled. Indoor plumbing! Thank goodness, the werewolves weren't completely medieval.

After using the restroom, I stared at my reflection in the bathroom mirror. I looked and felt tired. The stress of everything was beginning to weigh on me.

Another stall door opened and an attractive red-haired woman walked out of the stall. She stopped moving when she saw me and growled. "You!"

I looked around the bathroom before looking back at her. "Me?"

She snarled. "Why did he choose you? What makes you better than the rest of us?"

I frowned. "He didn't pick me. I'm his match. Plus, I never said I was better than you."

She jumped towards me with claws extended from where her fingernails used to be.

I jumped sideways and slammed my back against the wall. "I don't want to fight you!" I yelled as she came at me again.

She was swinging wildly and using only her claws. "I'll kill you and then he'll take me!" she yelled.

Koda threw open the door as the woman crouched to jump at me. He grabbed her around the waist and tossed her into one of the stalls. She hit her head against the back wall hard, stunning her. He rushed over to me and started running his hands over my face and shoulders. "Did she hurt you?"

I shook my head and batted his hands away. "I'm fine. She didn't touch me."

Koda turned to the woman who was holding her head in her hands and leaning against the wall of the stall he had thrown her into. "Attacking the prince's mate without challenge is illegal. Go visit the king after tonight's festivities," he said through clenched teeth.

The woman began sobbing.

Koda led me out of the bathroom and down the hallway. "I'm sorry, Artemis. I should have stayed with you."

I shook my head. "Nothing happened. I can take care of myself."

"I'm your guard, Artemis. It's my job to protect you," he said angrily.

I placed my hand on his arm, making him stop just before the door that led out to the main room. "Don't stress yourself over me. I can take care of myself. Besides, everyone dies some time. I don't want you blaming yourself if something out of your control happens."

He wrapped his arms around my shoulders. "I won't let

anything happen to you," he said seriously. Apparently, he wasn't willing to listen to reason.

He released me and pushed open the door. I stepped out into the main room and stared at the women surrounding Ares. One woman in a short skirt was sitting beside him, running her hand along his arm. My lip rose in a snarl, and I started to rush towards him.

Koda grabbed my arm, stopping me. "Artemis, calm down."

Ares looked away from the women and towards me. His smile disappeared when he saw my face.

I pulled against Koda's hold, but he held tight. "Let me go," I growled.

Koda shook his head. "Artemis, they aren't doing anything. They're just—"

"Flirting," I said angrily.

The women noticed Ares was looking away and followed his gaze. I snarled at them, and they all smiled. I pulled out of Koda's grip and walked towards the women, fuming. Ares stood and one of the women ran her hand down his chest. "Don't go. We were just starting to get back into the hang of things with you."

"Don't touch my mate!" I yelled at her.

"What are you going to do about it?" she asked with a smug smile on her face.

My hands started to heat up, and my body began glowing. "I swear if you touch him again, I'll rip your still beating heart from your chest."

The smile left her face, and her hand dropped away from Ares.

Ares rushed over to me and a wave of invisible fire knocked me backwards. "Calm down."

My body stopped glowing and my hands cooled.

Ares reached out towards, me and I took a step back, away from him. He frowned. "Artemis—"

One of the women spoke seductively. "Come on, Ares. Forget about that little girl and come play with us."

My anger was feeding the wolf in me, and I felt her eagerness to tear the girl apart with our claws. My body started to shudder and Ares grabbed my arm. "No."

I stopped shaking and glared at the women. "If any of you come near my mate again, I'll tear you apart."

Ares stroked my arm. "Artemis, nothing happened. We were all just talking."

I turned my gaze on him and saw him flinch. "Talking? I think the correct term is flirting."

Two women stood up from the table and started to walk towards us. One, a tall brunette who looked like a bull dog smiled evilly. "Why not let her fight to keep you? She doesn't deserve you, Ares. You deserve someone more beautiful, someone stronger."

I scoffed. "Look here, bull dog, I may be small, but I *know* I'm more beautiful than you *and* more powerful."

"Prove it," she said.

Ares released his hold on me and took two steps towards the girl. "Enough."

A woman two rows down leapt out of her seat, changing forms and shredding the skin tight dress she'd had on. She leapt at me, but I dodged, sliding to the right, and kicked her in the stomach. She yelped and landed on top of the table where the women were still sitting.

Achilles was a few seats down and stared at the wolf on the table next to him. "Always drama with the werewolves," he said quietly.

Two more females changed and started towards me from

behind. Koda grabbed one of the females, but the other one jumped around him and charged at me. I ripped Ares' necklace from my throat, putting it on the table next to me and changed forms in a matter of milliseconds. Luckily the dress was short enough that it didn't tear and only slid up underneath my front legs. The girl growled at me, and my ears pinned to my head. I leapt forward, dodging her outstretched paws and bit into her throat. Why was her guard down? Was she so consumed by jealousy that she wasn't thinking right? I tossed her to the side, missing Ares by inches.

Three more females from the table changed forms and Ares yelled, "Enough!"

The females stopped moving and stared at him.

I growled, and Ares turned to me, his eyes were golden wolf's eyes and his wolf looked at me from within him. "Be quiet." I stopped growling, but started walking down the aisle towards the exit. "Change back," Ares commanded.

My body twitched once and then changed back to human. Two tears leaked out of my eyes before I stood. Being forced to change was not a pleasant experience. I continued walking down the aisle, away from the women and Ares. A woman stepped out in front of me and Ares yelled, "Stop!"

The woman's body instantly stilled. I couldn't move my legs for a moment, but I pushed through the command he had given and took one slow step at a time. A black-haired woman jumped at me, but I punched her in the chest, knocking the wind out of her and making her stumble backwards to fall on her butt. Ares growled and all of the woman cowered. They seemed to finally decide to obey him. The steps were becoming easier, the further away I got from Ares.

"Artemis," Ares said softly. The softness of his voice and

the request in them made me stop moving. "Don't leave," he whispered.

My entire body hurt, begging me to turn around and run to him, but I wouldn't do it. "I'm going home," I said softly. "When you're finished, please come home, too."

"Artemis—" he began, but then Koda shushed him.

I hurried out of the building and away from the stares of the hundreds of werewolves who had witnessed everything. The cool night air felt like I had jumped into a lake of ice. I gasped and turned towards home. A human servant ran out of a shed to the right, carrying a box of wine. Alcohol. Ares said I could get drunk if I drank enough. I ran towards the shed and took three bottles of wine out. I hadn't been drunk before, but the euphoric look my friends used to get was enticing. If I drank enough, maybe I could attain that. The cork was a pain, but I finally managed to get it. I guzzled the wine and the liquor warmed my stomach.

Carrying the two unopened bottles in my left arm, I took long drinks out of the open bottle with my right hand.

"Artemis," Koda called when he stepped out of the building. I ignored him, heading towards home. "Artemis, wait," he said softly.

I turned to him and took a long drink from the wine bottle. "What?" I asked between drinks.

"What are you doing?" He tried to grab the bottle from my hand, which was now empty. I let him take it and jogged down the road as I opened one of the other bottles and started drinking from it. "Artemis, give me the wine."

"No," I said as I jogged backwards, away from him.

Ares stepped out of the building and stared at me. "What are you doing?"

I took a long drink out of the bottle, keeping my eye on

Koda. "Drinking," I said through a hiccup. The bottle was empty, but I pretended to drink out of it again.

"Give me the bottle," Ares said calmly.

A smile crossed my lips as I tossed him the empty bottle and then ran down an alleyway as I tried to open the new bottle. "Artemis!" Koda and Ares called after me.

The bottle finally opened, and I guzzled the entire thing down just before Ares stepped in front of me. I tried to slide to a stop, but my reflexes weren't up to par. My foot slipped out from under me, and I fell on my butt, flinging the empty bottle of wine. Ares' hand shot out to the left as he caught the bottle. "Why are you doing this?" he asked. "I didn't do anything with them." He started to reach towards me and I scrambled backwards.

"They're right," I said as I backed down the alleyway.

Ares sighed. "Stop this. You're being childish."

The words stung worse than I had expected them to. I knew I was being childish, but for him to say it to me was worse than a slap in the face. Tears streamed down my face. "That's all I'll ever be to you, isn't it? A child. A stupid little girl who you got matched with."

Koda popped up behind me.

I squatted down and whispered, "I'll leave." Ares opened his mouth, and I jumped upwards as high as I could. Grabbing ahold of the roof, I swung upwards and started running on the rooftops back towards the shed.

"Artemis, *stop!*" Ares commanded.

My legs stopped moving just as I reached the edge of the house I was running on. I fell off of the house and hit the ground on my side. My arm crunched, and I screamed in pain. The pain released my body from Ares' power so I could move again. When I stood, my right arm hung limply beside me. Ares was coming around the corner, but I didn't want to see him yet. I ran the last few yards to the shed and grabbed another bottle of wine. There wasn't a way for me to pull the cork out with my hands now, but I improvised and grabbed the cork with my teeth to jerk it out. The cork tumbled out of my mouth, and I replaced it with the bottle, guzzling the liquor.

Ares took the bottle from my hand and chucked it at the ground, shattering it. "Stop this!" He grabbed my injured arm making me scream in pain.

Koda appeared behind him and growled.

Ares growled back. "I didn't know her arm was broken."

Koda stopped growling and stepped away from him.

Ares looked at my arm for a moment then sighed. "We need to set it."

The world started to spin from the mixture of pain and alcohol. My knees gave, and Ares caught me before I hit the ground. "Let me go. You don't want me. You should be with one of them…a woman."

"Shut up." He picked me up in his arms and the world spun more. "I love you, and you are a woman, a beautiful, pigheaded, wild, and crazy woman."

"Spinning," I said softly.

Ares started sprinting, and it took all of my willpower not to throw up on him. He set me on the floor of the bathroom in our house and pulled my hair back. Matt and Koda came into the bathroom and each placed a hand on me while I puked up everything in my stomach. The physical contact of my pack comforted me and soon the nausea and pain in my head disappeared. "So, alcohol can get me drunk."

Ares laughed softly. "Yes."

I stood, but my arm began throbbing. I whimpered in pain

and Ares stood up quickly. "We need to set your arm. It's going to hurt…"

Koda stood on my other side and took my hand in his. "It'll be over in a second."

Matt grabbed a roll of gauze from underneath the sink and stood in front of me. "Ready."

Ares lifted my arm up and pushed on a bone in my upper arm. I screamed and all three men growled. Matt wrapped my arm to my body with the gauze in seconds and then they all wrapped their arms around me, giving me a group hug. The pain lasted another thirty seconds and then disappeared. Ares licked my cheek in apology for hurting me, and I nuzzled his neck.

My arm began throbbing again and then felt normal. Matt unwrapped the gauze and smiled. "Healed," he said.

I stepped away from them and quickly brushed my teeth. "I'm sorry," I said softly as I turned around. Ares and I were the only ones left in the bathroom. I hadn't heard the others leave.

"Artemis, I love you and only you. I'm sorry for flirting with them. I shouldn't have done that."

I folded my arms across my chest as the first tear fell down my face. "No, you shouldn't have."

Ares opened his hand, which held my diamond heart necklace with its broken chain. "Do you not want this anymore?" he asked softly, without looking at me.

I rushed forward and quickly took the necklace and chain. "I didn't want one of the women to break it or make me lose it. I'm sorry, Ares."

He wiped the tear tracks off of my face. "You're so beautiful. Every eye was on you tonight. Did you know that?"

I laughed bitterly. "Lots of women were glaring daggers at me, if that's what you mean."

Ares kissed my lips, pulling up my desire for him. "Lots of the males were looking at you. So many of them longing just to do this." He kissed me again and ran a hand up my arm. "If I were weaker, I would have a lot of challenges for you."

"Lots of women want to challenge me for you. They all want you. They all have pasts with you. How can I compete against those beautiful women?" I said softly.

"They have *pasts* with me, but only you have my present and my future." He ran a hand along my side. "This dress looks fantastic on you." I unbuttoned his shirt and ran my hand along his chest. He whispered, "I can't wait to see how great the dress looks on the floor, too."

He picked me up by my butt and set me down on the counter. My heart rate tripled, and I kissed him fiercely. He started to push up my dress when someone cleared their throat. Ares growled loudly. "Leave."

He started kissing me again and the person said, "Stop!"

I recognized the voice as Achilles'. Ares pulled away from me and the sight of his golden wolf eyes in his human face startled me. He glared at Achilles who was standing in the bedroom doorway. "What do you want?"

"I want you to stop touching her," Achilles hissed. His body glowed softly, and his hands balled into fists at his side.

Ares growled. "She's my mate. That means I mate with her. Leave us."

Achilles took a step into the bedroom. "No. While we're deciding what to do, you agreed not to do anything."

"I didn't mean that I wouldn't mate with her!" Ares snapped.

"It's not fair for you to share her flesh when I can't," Achilles said through clenched teeth.

"She doesn't want to sleep with you. She *wants* to sleep with me!" Ares bellowed.

Achilles eyes filled with pain, and he turned them towards me. "Artemis…"

I turned away from him. "Ares, maybe he's—"

Ares glared at me. "You agree with him?"

I hopped down from the counter and touched his arm. I opened my mouth to say something, but the anger he was holding in flooded over me like a wave of fire, scolding my skin. I screamed and the world went black.

FOUR

I woke up surrounded by heat and the smell of forest and wolf fur. "Mm, warm," I said softly.

"Artemis!" Koda yelled next to me.

"Shush. Not so loud." I groaned.

"Artemis, open your eyes," Matt said.

I opened my eyes and looked at their concerned faces staring down at me. "What happened?"

Ares spoke from somewhere in the room, "I hurt you." His voice was laced with pain.

I slowly sat up and looked at him sitting on the floor across the room. Achilles stood beside Ares, glaring down at him.

Frowning, I said, "I don't understand. I remember you were mad at Achilles and I said that maybe he was right and then your anger washed over me and…that's all."

Achilles spoke through clenched teeth. "He couldn't control his emotions. Your words upset him, and he caused you to faint."

I slid off of the bed and walked towards Ares. He stood up and turned his face away from me. "I'm sorry," he said softly.

I reached out towards him, but ended up touching the wall. I turned around and found him standing in the bathroom doorway. "Ares, stop moving away from me. I'm not mad at you. Come here."

Ares shook his head. "No, I should have more control than this…"

I sprinted across the room and knocked him to the ground, sitting on his stomach. "There, much better." Ares turned his head away from me. I grabbed his face and turned it towards mine. "Ares! Stop doing this. I'm fine. Sure, you made me faint, but I'm fine. I forgive you."

Ares smiled and hugged me against his chest. "I am sorry. I love you," he said as he kissed my cheek.

I stood up, taking Ares' hand as he rose next to me.

Achilles gaped at me. "That's it? Just like that, you forgive him?"

I shrugged. "He didn't mean to hurt me. Plus, I can't stay mad at him for too long."

Ares kissed the back of my hand. "It's one of her many great traits. She forgives easily and in turn allows us to forgive ourselves easily."

I looked at Achilles and then at Ares. They looked similar. "So, do you want to tell me why you two hate each other?"

Achilles rolled his eyes. "I don't hate him. He hates me."

Ares growled. "I hate all of you, but you the most."

"Why?" I asked.

Achilles smiled. "Yes, why don't you tell her?"

Ares shook his head. "I don't want to discuss it right now. It's painful enough that you're here and trying to steal my mate from me."

"I'm not stealing her! She was mine before she was yours." Achilles ground out.

I stepped between them and held up my hands. "Stop bickering!" They both stared at me in shock as I groaned. "You're both acting like two spoiled kids fighting over a toy. I'm not a *toy*! I have feelings and opinions, and my opinion is that I don't know how I feel about Achilles. What I do know is that if we are honestly discussing the issues he has with us, then we need to be fair. Achilles, you have to understand that because of our bond I need the physical contact with Ares. Now, can you two not try to fight each other and just..." I stopped talking as a wave of fear rolled over me. I turned away from the men and ran towards the window that looked out over the forest behind the village. Dark shapes darted between the trees one hundred or so yards out. "Ares!" I said urgently.

Ares rushed to my side and looked out the window. He growled loudly. "Koda, warn the town. Achilles protect the house. Matt, protect the village," Ares ordered. The men didn't hesitate. Each one ran to do his job.

I looked at Ares. "What are we going to do?"

He picked me up in his arms. "We're going to hide and keep you safe."

I shook my head. "No! Ares, the town needs you to help protect them. You're the prince for a reason."

Ares turned his head so I couldn't look at his face. "I can't."

"What? Why not?" I asked, confused.

"I can't...I can't lose you again," he said softly.

I turned his face to look at mine. "Ares, you have to protect the children. I can fight."

Ares shook his head. "No. You can't fight. I won't let you

be taken from me again." He kissed my cheek and laid his head against mine.

"Ares," I whispered. "You have a duty to protect your village. Let Koda protect me, or Matt, or even Achilles."

Ares growled. "Not Achilles."

Matt ran up the stairs. "There's a group of twenty dhampirs and ten vampires surrounding the village. I smelled ogres, too, but haven't seen them. What do you want us to do? Do we try to talk to them?"

Ares looked at me and sighed. "Matt, guard Artemis. I'll go." I kissed Ares' cheek and smiled. Ares looked at Matt. "Don't let anything happen to her."

Matt nodded and held out his arms. "I swear."

Ares set me in Matt's arms and walked towards the bedroom door.

"I love you, Ares," I said softly.

Ares turned around and smiled. "I love you, too." He disappeared from my sight and I heard the front door open and close.

Matt set me on my feet. "We're going to stay in here. Achilles will keep them from coming in downstairs and if you're here by the bathroom I can keep them away from you if they get to the second story."

"So, you want me to hide in the bathroom?" I asked, narrowing my eyes at him.

Matt clenched his teeth. "My job is to keep you safe and keeping you in this room, where they have the least access to you, is the best way to do that."

"I can fight, Matt," I hissed.

Matt smiled. "I know, Love, but I need you safe more than I need to help your ego today. Just stay there and hide if I tell you to."

I groaned, but walked to the bathroom doorway and sat down. "I hope none of the children get hurt. Why would dhampirs and vampires be attacking us if we're allies?"

"I'm not sure." He turned away from me to look out the window nearest him. His answer seemed off, like he was hiding something.

Snarling, growling, and screaming, slowly filled the air. Matt paced from one window to the other as the sounds of fighting grew closer and closer to us. A window shattered downstairs.

I started to get up, but Achilles called up to us, "It's fine. He's dead."

Matt continued his pacing. He suddenly stopped and cussed. "Shit. Achilles, they're swarming us."

Matt ran to me and picked me up in his arms.

"What are you doing?" I squealed.

"I was wrong. We can't hide you. We need to run," Matt said as he ran from the bedroom down the stairs. He was talking so quickly that his British accent was making it difficult for me to understand him. "Achilles, they're coming for her."

Achilles blinked at me for a moment before answering, "Let me take her. I can fly her up away from them."

Matt shook his head. "No, Ares doesn't want you touching her. Just follow us. I need to get her away from here."

Achilles opened his mouth to argue, but the front door splintered as someone ran through it. A short black man stood in the doorway glaring at us. "Give me the girl, and we'll leave you alone," he said slowly.

Matt growled. "Not a chance, dhampir."

Achilles' body began to glow and then he shot blue fireballs from his hands at the dhampir. The dhampir ran to the right to avoid the fire, and Matt dashed through the door and out of the house. Ten men rushed towards us from the tree line. I spotted Ares across the town, fighting with a vampire. It surprised me that Ares was still in human form, but the vampire didn't look like he was giving Ares too much trouble. Ares turned his head, noticing me and started running towards us.

Matt ran towards the heart of the town. Ares caught up to us and yelled, "What are you doing? Why did you bring her out here?"

Matt didn't look at Ares as he ran towards the castle in the center of the town. "They're coming for her, Ares. They were swarming the house. I couldn't keep her there. She'll be safer away from the edges of the forest where they're coming from."

Ares ran beside us as Matt rushed into the castle and into a room that had no windows and only one door. Matt set me down in the back corner. "Stay here," he said sternly.

Ares smiled at me and then they both ran out of the room, leaving me alone. I knew it was stupid, but I was worried about Ares. Just the thought of him being hurt or killed brought tears to my eyes. The sounds of fighting were still loud, but I couldn't figure out who was winning.

Why was my life so crazy now? It felt like years had passed since I was with my little human pack of Bret and Billy and their friends. I gasped as I realized why Darren had allowed me and Bret to be alone all that time and sleep in the same bed together. He knew that I wouldn't have wanted to mate with Bret, that he was just a pack mate to me. It made sense that I had craved physical contact even if it was from humans since I was, by nature, a pack animal. It would have been a lot easier on me if I'd known all of that back then though.

"What do we have here?" asked a female voice. I turned and looked at the doorway where an ugly woman with black hair and alabaster skin stood, smiling at me. "Now, why would they hide a girl in this room? You must be special for them to want to protect you."

"Leave if you value your life." I growled and stood with my back to the wall.

She laughed. "You don't scare me, girl. I bet you're the one all this commotion is over, aren't you?" She walked slowly towards me, her fingers elongating into six-inch daggers.

Fear consumed me. "I don't know what you're talking about." The words came out weak instead of strong as I'd hoped.

"I can't believe your mate would leave you unguarded like this. He must be overly cocky to think you'd be safe." She stopped twenty feet away from me and closed her eyes. Her face shifted and the ugly woman turned into a hideous monster with fangs and a distorted face. "I'm hungry, let's finish this."

She jumped at me, and I shot a purple fireball at her. I only had a moment to enjoy the color of the fireball, which matched my eyes, before she jumped to the side, my fireball only grazing her. She dropped to the ground and smacked the spot where the fire had caught on her clothes. She extinguished the flame, screamed in rage and charged at me. I lobed ball after ball of fire at her as she ran towards me, but she dodged them all. The daggers of her right hand jammed into my side making me scream.

"You were never meant to live. It's sad your mate chose you because now he'll have to deal with your death!" She jammed her other set of dagger-fingers into my stomach and smiled as I screamed again.

My skin began glowing brighter and brighter, until the vampire hissed and pulled her daggers from me. The anger I'd been holding in since I'd met Ares boiled to the top and spilled over. My skin glowed white and all logical thoughts left my mind. *Kill. Kill the vampire.* Lunging at the vampire, I grabbed onto her shirt and rode her body down to the ground. My right hand became covered in fire.

The vampire screamed, "Please. Mercy."

"You weren't going to give me mercy, so you shall receive none." The words came from my mouth and it was as though my wolf and I became one in that instant. No longer was it my wolf and me, but it was me and the animal instincts, urges, and thoughts, together. In one swift motion I plunged my fire covered hand into her chest and ripped her heart out. She screamed long and loud as I held her heart in my hand. The sounds were annoying.

I repositioned myself so that I was sitting above her head to get into a better spot. The heart had begun to blister from the fire in my hand, and long black smears surrounded it. With one quick squeeze of my hand, the heart turned to ash and sifted to the floor beside the vampire's head. Her scream turned into a high-pitched shriek. Ares appeared in the doorway and gaped at me as I picked her head up off the floor, gave one violent twist, and tore her head from her body.

The screaming stopped, and my anger dissipated. I dropped the head onto the ground, turned and vomited.

"It's alright, Artemis. Everything's alright now," Ares said softly as he stroked my hair.

I looked at my hands, expecting them to be covered in blood, but surprisingly they were clean. My wounds however were still open and blood poured from them, staining my white dress. "Ares, my wounds," I whispered as I started to faint.

Ares picked me up and ran. I faded in and out of consciousness, closer to out, than in. Ares kept talking to me, "Artemis, Sunshine, stay awake."

"I am awake. I'm awake and in pain. Where did you go?" I asked.

"I was protecting the front entrance to the castle. Matt was supposed to be protecting the back," he said through gritted teeth.

"Is he hurt?"

Ares shook his head. "He's not dead at least. I would have felt it if he had died."

Our house came into view as did Koda and Achilles. Ares set me on the porch and a beautiful blonde haired, blue eyed woman stepped out of the house wearing an apron. Who was she? Where had she come from? "What's happened?" she asked.

Ares ripped my dress off and everyone gasped. The woman knelt down beside me and started wiping the blood off of my stomach and side. "You're going to be alright. She didn't hit any vital organs and they're already beginning to heal."

Ares held my hand as she started chanting in a different language. "You did well against the vampire. I'm proud of you," he said softly.

His compliment made me smile. "Thanks."

The woman stopped and sat back on her heels, a bead of sweat rolling down her face. "She's fine, Ares. Your anger is becoming too much, please calm down," she whispered.

Ares took a deep breath and kissed my forehead. "I'm sorry, Gwen."

Gwen smiled. "I've never seen you so worried over a female before, or so gentle. She must be your mate."

Ares nodded and picked me up in his arms. "She is. Thank you again for your services, Gwen."

Gwen bowed her head. "Anytime, Prince."

Ares carried me into the house, up the stairs and to the bathroom. He set me down on the toilet seat and then turned on the shower. I watched him as he silently moved about the bathroom. He was bothered about something. My wounds were almost fully healed now, so I stood up and approached Ares, who stood beside the now warm water of the shower.

He turned to look at me, tears in his eyes.

"Ares, what is it?" I asked as I wiped the tears from his face and kissed each cheek.

He wrapped his arms around me and exhaled loudly. "I almost lost you again."

"Ares, I wasn't that close to dying. You heard Gwen—she missed the vital organs. Look, the wounds are already sealed." I grabbed his hand and placed it on my stomach where one of the wounds had been.

He ran his fingertip over the small pink scar that was quickly disappearing. "I'm sorry I failed you," he said softly.

"You didn't fail me. You were protecting one entrance while Matt was supposed to be protecting the other. How could you have known something would happen to Matt?" I pulled his shirt off over his head and kissed his chest. "Help me wash," I said as seductively as I could.

A smile lifted the right corner of his mouth and he unbuttoned his pants. "Alright."

I turned away from him and stepped underneath the water. The warm water felt good on my skin and helped erase the shock that was trying to set in. Ares began scrubbing my body with a soap bar, paying special attention to the blood on my stomach and side. He kissed my neck and turned me around underneath the water to rinse off.

For once, I wasn't overcome by my hormones and my desire to sleep with him, but instead the touch and caring fulfilled my needs. It was amazing to be loved like this. I hoped it never ended. He turned me around to face him and kissed my lips softly. "I love you, Artemis."

I kissed his lips and then rested my head against his chest. "I love you, too." Ares wrapped his arms around me and sighed.

"Excuse me." a female said softly.

My hackles, figuratively, rose, and I turned to the doorway, snarling. The young girl flinched and took a step back. "Sorry," I said softly.

Ares grabbed two towels and wrapped his around his waist. I wrapped mine around my body. "What is it, Lauren?" Ares asked in a soft voice.

"Darius wishes to speak to you, immediately," she said in a soft voice. Her strawberry blonde hair was naturally curly and hid her face from my view.

"I'll put pants on and be there in a moment. Wait downstairs for me," Ares said. Lauren curtsied and then rushed out of the room. Ares whispered, "She seems innocent, but she's been Darius' assistant for twenty years. I wouldn't be surprised if she was as cunning as he is."

I adjusted my towel. "I'm glad you're the one that has to deal with all of the political crap. I couldn't even stand listening to people in town debating about the presidential elections. Boring."

Matt walked in and smiled at us. "Who's boring?"

Ares blurred as he moved from the shower to the door in

an instant to grab Matt around the throat. "Where did you go? You were supposed to be protecting the back entrance!" Ares yelled.

Matt's lip twitched for a moment as though he were thinking about snarling and then he whined. "Sorry. I saw two vampires attacking a child and so I went to help, but then got ambushed." He looked towards me and asked, "Did something happen?"

Ares released Matt's throat. "Artemis was attacked."

Matt looked at me with an almost sad look on his face. "Are you alright?" Was he sad I was attacked or that I survived?

I nodded. "I'm fine."

Matt smiled. "Good."

Ares looked at Matt a moment longer before yelling, "Koda!" Koda ran into the bathroom and looked at our faces. Ares looked at me. "Koda, guard Artemis."

Koda nodded, and Matt walked out of the room with Ares. "What happened?" Koda asked.

"Nothing," I said as I walked to the closet to change.

Koda leaned against the doorframe while I changed clothes. "Achilles said you used your Sidhe powers to fight the vampire."

I looked up at him in shock. "How did he know that?"

Koda smiled. "We can feel magic from those of our kind when they're being used in significant enough quantities. He said it's been a long time since he felt such a large pull."

"Well, she was trying to kill me," I said defensively as I buttoned my pants.

"Ares is having Victor come here to speak with Darius about this attack. They swear that it wasn't a sanctioned attack, and that they had no idea it was going to happen."

I looked at Koda's tight face. "You don't believe them?"

Koda smiled. "I believe Victor, but I'm not sure about Maurice."

Matt's attitude and response still bothered me, so I decided to tell Koda. After I'd finished Koda sighed. "I've been noticing it, too," he said quietly. "Something's bothering him, but I'm not sure what it is."

"Do you think he lied about why he stopped guarding the back entrance?" That part was bothering me the most. I couldn't explain why, but I knew he was lying about why he left.

Koda sighed and ran a hand through his Mohawk which I noticed wasn't gelled up for once. "I don't know. I'll have to speak to Ares about it." He looked at my face for a moment before sighing. "Come on, you should lie down. You've had a lot happen to you."

I laughed and climbed onto the bed. "I never thought my life would be so crazy."

Koda laid down beside me and rubbed my back. "Don't worry, things will calm down, and we'll be able to show you the good side of life as a werewolf."

"I can't wait for that day," I mumbled as I relaxed and took comfort in Koda's touch. "Thank you," I whispered as I started to lose consciousness.

"For what?" he asked.

"For being you."

"Artemis?"

"Night, Koda."

The sun rose earlier than I wanted, but waking up to Ares' arms wrapped around me definitely made it better.

"Morning, Sunshine," Ares whispered against my neck.

I shivered and asked, "Can't we sleep in?"

Ares chuckled and nipped my ear. "We need to go on a hunt. Come on. Everyone is waiting for you."

I groaned and rolled over until my face was pressed against Ares'. "I think we should stay in bed all day." I opened my eyes and stared at the handsome man looking at me. "You're too handsome for me," I sighed longingly.

Ares kissed my lips and rolled us over until he was lying on top of me. "Achilles left a couple minutes ago. He won't be able to tell that we've mated if we do it before the hunt."

He started kissing his way down my neck and it took all of my willpower to form conscious thoughts. "Ares, I thought you said Koda and Matt were waiting?"

"They can wait a little longer." He growled as he tried to work my shirt up.

"Ares, I know you don't like Achilles, but it really isn't fair. What if the situation was flipped and he'd claimed me first? What would you want him to do?"

Ares groaned and pressed his forehead against mine. "Fine, but we need to figure out a solution soon. It's torment to be near you and not be able to mate with you."

I kissed his cheek softly. "I know. It's hard for me, too, but we'll figure something out."

I climbed out from under Ares and hopped down from the bed. It took my body a moment to change, but it was painless when I finally took my wolf form.

Matt and Koda yelled through my head. *Hurry up!*

I jogged down the stairs and opened my mouth in a wolf-grin at the two giant wolves sitting on the porch. *Morning.*

Ares walked out in front of me. *Come on, let's hunt. I need to kill something.*

I giggled, but the strange wheezing sound that came out of my wolf throat bothered me too much to continue. Ares glared at me with a tight mouth. *That'll teach you to laugh at me.*

Ares jogged away from the house and the rest of us followed behind him as he led us into the forest. We jogged for twenty minutes before smelling another animal. I twitched my nose in frustration. *What is it?* I couldn't figure out what animal I was smelling.

Deer. Ares said. He tilted his head to the right then turned to face in that direction. *There.*

We all turned slowly and stared at the herd of deer two hundred yards away. A ten point buck stood a little to the side of the herd. My mouth instantly started watering. Ares snorted softly, and Matt and Koda took off at a run. I started to follow, but Ares blocked my path. *Watch. You need to learn how to take down a buck first.*

Matt snapped at the buck's heels and Koda grabbed onto the distracted buck's throat. In only a few seconds they'd killed the buck. Ares trotted over and started eating. I sat down beside Matt and Koda who were sitting a few feet away.

Ares finished and looked at us. *Artemis eats next.* Matt growled and Ares growled back, his lips pulling up in a menacing snarl. *I'm alpha. I decide when my mate eats. She eats after me. You and Koda decide who eats after that.*

Matt stopped growling and then snorted in irritation. I trotted forward and took a bite out of the deer. *It's delicious!* It took only a minute for me to fill up on the deer. I licked my muzzle clean and trotted over to Ares who was licking one of his paws clean. *That was great.*

Ares licked my cheek. *Glad you like it.*

Matt whined. *There's another herd up ahead.*

Ares nodded once. *Let's go. This time, I take down the buck.*

Koda, Matt and Ares took off running before I could react. I watched as Ares ran, his muscles stretching and his fur pressed against his body. The buck lifted his head from the grass he was eating and then Ares was on him. I walked slowly towards the rest of my pack and laid down in a sunny spot a few yards away from the dead buck. *That was great.* I said quietly as Ares ate.

Koda snorted. *You're easily impressed.*

Ares finished eating and nodded at me.

I'm full. Thanks. I lifted my lips in a grin and rolled on to my back so the sun could warm my stomach. *We should have done this sooner.*

Ares laid down, placing his head on top of my stomach. *I'll make sure we take more time to hunt together.*

Matt walked towards us, and I felt uneasy, not wanting to be on my back anymore. I rolled over and sat up next to Ares.

Matt looked at me quizzically, but didn't say anything as he sat down and waited for Koda to finish.

I was still bothered by Matt's lie and in wolf form I especially felt awkward around him. Ares draped his head across my neck and sighed in contentment. *How are you feeling today?*

Fine, thank you. I said quietly as I enjoyed his warmth and the smell of his fur. I noticed another slightly different, but familiar smell underneath Ares' fur, against his skin, but I couldn't place it.

Koda trotted over, licking his lips clean. *Okay, I'm done.*

Ares pulled away, and we all ran back towards the house. I changed forms at the door and ran inside and up the stairs. I stepped into the bedroom and stopped in my tracks. A slim, beautiful black-haired woman was lying, naked on the bed.

She sat up when I walked in and glared at me. "Where is Ares?"

I growled loudly and squatted down, preparing to attack. "Why are you on my bed, naked?"

She stood and glared at me. "I do not need to speak to you, *girl*. I came to see the prince. Now, step aside."

Ares walked up behind me and stared in shock at the woman. "Natasha? What are you doing here?"

She smiled seductively and posed against the bed post. "I was waiting for you."

I growled again, and Ares sighed. "Oh. I see. Natasha, you need to leave."

Natasha's beautiful smile wilted as she looked from me to Ares. "You would reject me for this…this *child*?"

Koda walked up the stairs and pulled me backwards, away from Natasha. Apparently, he guessed I was about to pounce on her.

Ares took a step towards Natasha and speaking in a

soothing tone said, "You need to leave, Natasha. This is not your home, nor is this your pack. Leave."

She stuck out her bottom lip in a pout and took a step closer to Ares, running a fingertip over his chest. "Ares, you know you would rather have me."

Anger boiled up in me, tinting my sight red. I wanted to change forms, but I held the change and instead charged at Natasha, knocking her to the ground and punching her in the face before Ares pulled me away. "Let me go!" I yelled as I struggled to attack her again.

Koda knelt down beside Natasha's still body and then turned to smile at me. "You knocked her out cold. I'm impressed."

Ares wrapped his arms around me and exhaled. His magic wrapped around me like the warm hug he was holding me in and calmed me. "Artemis, relax. You know I would never, could never, cheat on you. Especially not with a trashy woman like Natasha."

I turned around slowly and asked, "Is she one of your former flings?"

"Yes, but I never felt anything for her."

Natasha moaned and sat up. "You bitch. You'll pay for that."

Koda picked Natasha up and started carrying her downstairs. "Time to go."

Natasha struggled against him, but decided instead to turn towards me. "You don't deserve Ares! You don't deserve to be in this pack. I challenge you. Accept, you *coward.*"

Ares opened his mouth to speak, but I spoke up before he could. "A challenge for what?"

Her eyes brightened happily. Ares shook his head, Koda's

mouth gaped, and Achilles walked inside the front door, staring at our group.

Natasha pulled out of Koda's arms and glared at me. "A fight to the death. Winner gets Ares and his pack."

"Artemis, stop this, you can't—" Ares began.

"I accept," I said over Ares' words.

Ares stared at me in complete and utter shock, as did Achilles and Koda.

Natasha nodded. "In three days at noon, meet me at the fountain." She winked at Ares and then jogged out of the house.

Ares' anger had been building since I had accepted and as soon as she was gone, he turned on me and yelled, "What are you thinking? Do you realize what you just did?"

He'd never been mad at me before, and it took all of my courage not to cower. "I'm protecting my place. None of the women here believe I should have you as a mate. I've been attacked and insulted, and I'm tired of it. I'm going to prove, once and for all, that I'm your mate and I'll die to keep that title."

Ares roared, "Did you think what would happen if you lose?" He stormed down the stairs without looking at me again.

Achilles was glowing and glaring at Ares. "You let her accept?"

Ares moved faster than my eye could track and suddenly had Achilles pinned to the wall of the entryway. "I did not let her! She did it herself!"

Achilles shoved Ares back, flinging him into the other wall. "You should have stopped her!"

Ares screamed and charged at Achilles, who charged at him, glowing brighter and brighter. The sound of their hits was like a jack hammer on concrete and soon I was covering my ears. Koda and Matt rushed into the fight and tried, unsuccessfully, to stop them. The metallic taste of blood hit my tongue from the air, and my senses finally returned. I rushed down the stairs and threw my self between the two men. Ares' fist stopped an inch away from my face and both men took a few steps away from me.

"Stop it. Both of you! I chose this and none of you could have stopped me. Stop fighting." The words came out loud and strong, like a drill sergeant ordering their cadets. I looked from one angry set of eyes to another and noticed that both had a split lip, but no other damage seemed present. "Please, don't fight."

Ares growled and stormed out of the house, walking towards the forest. Matt jogged after him silently. Achilles walked away from me and towards the room where he was staying. My legs started to give and only my arm reaching out and hitting the wall saved me. Koda rushed forward and picked me up. "Artemis?"

"I messed up, didn't I?" I asked in a small voice.

Koda nuzzled my cheek. "They're just worried." Koda shut the front door and walked up the stairs, keeping a tight grip on me.

"Are you mad at me, too?"

He kept looking straight ahead, avoiding looking at my face. "I don't think you should have accepted her challenge and I'm worried about the consequences. I am not mad at you though. Just worried."

"Is she that strong?" I asked nervously.

"She's one of the strongest females." He set me down and pushed me towards the bathroom. "Go take a shower. I'll keep guard."

I groaned as I started walking towards the shower. "It's ridiculous that I have a guard. I'm capable of protecting myself. I'm not a helpless female in need of a big man to protect me all of the time." Sure, sometimes it was nice to have backup, like when vampires and dhampirs attacked, but I could hold my own.

"Complaining won't change anything. No matter what you say, Ares is going to keep a guard on you."

The shower head groaned for a minute before turning on. My body suddenly felt very cold and the steam rising from the shower head was more than inviting. "Do you think Ares is going to come back?" I asked as I stepped into the shower and relaxed under the hot water.

"He'll come back. He's just blowing off some steam." Koda assured me.

I quickly showered and then dried my hair. Outside, a large crash sounded, making me jump. Koda rushed over and picked me up in his arms.

"Put me down, Koda. Why do you guys always pick me up and carry me? I'm not an invalid."

Koda set me on my feet and frowned down at me. "We pick you up because, as you're aware, touch helps soothe us when we're feeling upset. Plus, it's more effective to pick you up and hold you while we run somewhere to protect you."

"I'm sorry. I didn't mean to snap at you," I said softly.

Koda kissed my cheek. "It's alright. I forgive you. It was probably just Ares knocking over a tree anyways. Come on, we better get dressed so we can start training."

"Training? For what?"

He turned to me and all of the humor that usually lit Koda's eyes was gone, leaving them a dull blue. "You have to train for your fight. I won't lose my pack mate just because we were mad at you and didn't train you properly."

I followed Koda to the room and quickly dressed in jeans and a t-shirt. He dressed in only a pair of sweats and shook his head at me when I reached for shoes. "I need to teach you some tricks about changing to your wolf form. Put some sweats on instead."

"Ares didn't buy me any sweats," I whispered, feeling Ares' absence like a weight on my shoulders.

Koda handed me a pair of his sweats. "Cinch the string as tight as it will go on your waist and then roll the waistband so the legs are shorter for you."

I did as he suggested and then followed him back down the stairs. As we opened the front door to leave, Achilles walked out of his room. "Where are you going?"

"I'm taking her to the woods to do some training." Koda answered.

Achilles was frowning hard, but only a faint line creased his perfect brow. "I'll accompany you."

Koda looked like he wanted to object, but shrugged instead and pushed me towards the door. "Come on. We've only got three days to train you."

The three of us walked in silence through the woods. I felt nervous, but I knew Koda wouldn't hurt me. Although, I wasn't sure of Achilles' intentions, but I doubted he would hurt me either. Koda led us to a small circular clearing filled with grass and wild flowers. It was beautiful and yet I could smell dried blood on the ground. "This is our training field," Koda explained to me. He walked to the center of the clearing and motioned at me to come towards him. "I want you to attack me, but do not use your Sidhe powers, or change to your complete wolf form."

I nodded and walked to stand a few feet away from him. I took two deep cleansing breaths before moving forward as fast as I could and punching at Koda. He spun around me and, in an instant, had an arm wrapped around my throat, choking me. "You're too slow. You need to move faster. You also need to pay more attention to your opponent. As soon as you see me moving to go behind you, you should turn. Again."

For the next few hours, Koda drilled me again and again. He then started teaching me how to properly hit and kick and then how to use my elbows. My body was sore, and I was dripping with sweat when he said, "Now I'm going to teach you to half-shift."

Achilles stood from the spot in the grass where he had been sitting. "She's not ready for that."

Koda ignored Achilles and in a blink of an eye his body changed from Koda the man to Koda the man-wolf. His body was bulkier, but he could still walk on two legs, his hands were now paws and his entire body was covered in short fur. His face was more wolfish with a slight snout instead of just a nose and fangs in his mouth. It took him two tries before he could speak and when he did it sounded more like a growl than a human voice. "This is the best form to take when fighting because you have the benefits of the wolf strength while still being able to move on two legs. It's difficult to maintain though and so most of us prefer to simply take wolf form." He changed back to his human shape and leaned forward a little. "I need to practice more often. I'm getting rusty." He shook his entire body, like a dog flinging off water and waved his hand at me. "Your turn."

"How do I take that shape instead of my wolf shape?" I asked. Usually I just closed my eyes and let the wolf side of me take over to become wolf, or pictured my human self to become human.

"You just focus on keeping half your body human."

My body began to tingle all over in anticipation of changing. *Okay, only change part way.* I felt my bones shifting and then opened my eyes, but I was on all fours and, after wagging my tail realized, a complete wolf.

Koda shrugged. "We'll keep working on it. It's hard to do."

I changed back and sighed. "I'm sorry."

Koda smiled. "Don't be. Only a few are able to master this technique. Come on, let's get you some food."

Achilles followed behind us as we walked back to the house. Why had he come? He hadn't talked except when he thought I wasn't ready to learn the half-shift. Was he just worried about me? Was he spying on me? I shook my head and ignored all of the questions. I wouldn't know unless I asked, but I didn't want to. He still unnerved me in that weird, good way and I wasn't sure how to feel about that.

Ares stood on the front porch with Matt when we came up. He looked at my sweat covered body and ripped sweats and then at Koda's ripped sweats. "What were you doing?"

Koda smiled sweetly at Ares. "Nothing."

Ares frowned at Koda, but didn't press him further. I walked past him, knowing he was still mad and continued to the kitchen where Koda had already taken out three steaks. I sat down on one of the stools at the island and laid my face on the cold tile. "I'm sore."

Koda laughed. "Good."

I whispered, "Am I supposed to keep what we do a secret from Ares?"

Koda shook his head. "No, I just like irking him."

Ares walked in and looked from me to Koda. "What are you two whispering about?"

Koda turned on the stove top and put oil in a pan. "How I should prepare the meat."

Ares rolled his eyes. "You're the worst liar I know."

The closeness of Ares, but lack of touch made my skin itch. It'd been hours since we'd had physical contact, and I needed it bad. My arm started to reach out towards him, but I quickly pulled it back and closed my eyes. I didn't want to push him if he was mad at me.

He sat down beside me and when I opened my eyes, I found his head lying on the island next to me. "Are you feeling alright?" he asked.

"Tired," I whispered as a lump formed in my throat. The sight of his handsome face still sent butterflies whirling in my stomach.

He frowned for a second and then exhaled loudly before putting one of his arms around my shoulders. "Aw. Much better. Wasn't your skin tingling?"

"As if one thousand ants were crawling on it," I said honestly.

He moved his face closer to mine. "Then why didn't you touch me?"

I closed my eyes before answering. "You're mad at me. I didn't want to make you angrier by trying to touch you. I was letting you decide when we touched again."

He kissed my nose, shocking me and making me open my eyes. "Artemis, if you need to touch me, then touch me. If you need me to hug you, then tell me. No matter how mad at you I may be, I don't want you to suffer."

My shoulders relaxed and after scooting my stool closer to his, I rubbed my cheek against his. "Thank you."

Koda cleared his throat. I pulled away from Ares and took the plate Koda was holding out to me. Koda sat on the stool across the island from me and ate his food in silence, keeping his gaze down. Ares handed me a knife and fork and I quickly cut up the meat. Ares put his arm around my waist and I ate with my two favorite men. I tried to offer Ares a piece of the steak, but he just shook his head.

When the steak was gone, I leaned against Ares and sighed in contentment. "I love you both."

Ares kissed the top of my head and Koda smiled at me.

"Where's Matt?" I asked curiously.

Ares exhaled. "With a female, I believe. He asked for leave and since I don't need to go anywhere and I don't *actually* need a guard, I let him go."

Koda shook his head. "Something's not right with him. He's been different since we came back from the vampires' place."

Ares nodded. "I know. I've been trying to figure out what's different, but I don't know."

"Ares?"

"Hm."

"How'd you get the name 'God of War'?" I asked. I'd been wondering about it since the men who had kidnapped me for the vampire queen had discussed it.

I smelled Achilles as he walked to stand by the kitchen entrance. Ares shrugged and then said, "I was a good warrior and, because of my genetics, to the humans I appeared as a god."

Achilles scoffed from the doorway. "You withhold much from her. Why?"

Ares growled. "Go away, *Sidhe*." He said "Sidhe" with such malice that it made me pull away from him.

Achilles was rubbing his temples. "This hatred you have towards me is wrongfully placed. It was not my fault."

Ares stood and growled louder. "It *was* your fault! You could have prevented it! Instead you sat by and let it happen!" Ares had gone from irritated to ready to kill in two seconds.

"What happened?" I asked softly.

Ares shook his head and turned away. "I won't discuss it." He held out his hand towards me. I looked at him for a moment before realizing that he was playing a power game with Achilles. He wanted me to put my hand in his so Achilles got the hint that I was Ares' and Achilles couldn't do anything about it.

"Ares, why do you hide so much from me? I'm your mate." I whispered the words so that he wouldn't take them as a challenge.

His eyes glistened as though covered with a film of unshed tears. "This is not a topic I wish to discuss. Maybe at some point I will talk with you about it, but not now and not while *he* is here."

"You're just as stubborn as Father," Achilles said angrily.

Ares spun around and glared at Achilles, baring his teeth. "I have *no* father!" Spinning on his heel, Ares marched out of the kitchen and stomped up the stairs. I looked at Achilles apologetically and rushed up the stairs to the room where I found Ares staring out the window at the woods. "I'm sorry, Artemis. That was childish of me," he said quietly.

I wrapped my arms around him from behind and lay my head against his back. "Achilles does an excellent job of upsetting you."

Ares laughed softly and turned around to hug me. "That he does. So, what were you and Koda really doing?"

"Koda's training me," I answered honestly.

Ares grip tightened and his words came out clipped. "So. You're still going forward with the challenge?"

I nodded.

"You could die, you know this?"

I nodded again.

He pushed me back gently and looked at my face. "Why then? Why are you doing this?"

"I have to prove myself, Ares. Since I've met you, you all have been fighting for me and protecting me. It's time that I protect myself and prove to the rest of the pack that I'm not helpless."

Ares relaxed his grip and sighed loudly. "You could have just battled someone. You didn't have to do a fight to the death that would result in forcing a new mate on me if you lose."

"She challenged me, Ares. I couldn't refuse. Would you have refused if it were a man challenging you for me?"

Ares laughed softly. "No, I suppose I wouldn't have, but then again, I'm a veteran at fighting. You aren't."

I rubbed my sore shoulders. "I know."

Ares poked my shoulder, making me wince. "Come on, let's get you into the nice spa."

"Mm, the spa sounds wonderful," I said wistfully. Ares laughed and steered me towards the bathroom. He started the water while I stripped out of my dirty clothes. It hurt to raise my arms above my head, but I got my shirt off with only a little groaning. Ares tested the water in the giant spa and then stripped out of his own clothes. He climbed into the spa and held out his hand to help me in. I let him help me as I climbed into the hot water and then slid down against the wall of the spa, sighing happily.

Ares moved to sit down beside me and held one of my hands in his. "I love you, Artemis."

I snuggled against him as the hot water relaxed my sore muscles. "I love you, too. Have you thought of any ways to get Achilles to give up?"

Ares shook his head. "No. You?"

"No."

We sat in comfortable silence as we enjoyed the closeness of each other and the pleasantness of our contact. My eyes started to droop closed when Ares leapt out of the spa and growled loudly. I spun around and stared in shock at a woman with a dagger pinned against the wall by Ares. She struggled against his hold, her eyes fixed on me. "Female! Female, look at me!" Ares yelled at her, but she didn't take her eyes off of me or stop trying to get away from him. He closed his eyes for a second before shaking his head. "She's turning."

"Turning into what?" I asked.

"Turning rogue. Her wolf is taking control of her even in her human body. Artemis, run downstairs and stay there. Tell Koda to come here."

I obeyed Ares' instructions and ran down the stairs. Koda rushed up the stairs. "I just noticed the front door was open. We didn't even hear it."

I pointed up. "Ares has a woman who tried to stab me. He says she's turning rogue."

Koda cursed and ran up the stairs. Achilles walked towards me with a white robe in his hands.

I quickly put it on. "They have to kill her, don't they?" I asked Achilles.

Achilles nodded. "Yes. If you are of a foul mind and you let the wolf take over, you will kill whatever is in your path. Your own children included."

I looked at him curiously. "You talk as if you are one."

He shrugged. "I lived among the wolves for a number of years. I've seen a rogue attack twice. It is not something you easily forget."

The woman screamed and then the house was eerily silent. I shuddered at the knowledge that Ares or Koda had killed her. Even if it was necessary, it unnerved me. "Artemis, go in the kitchen and make us some dinner, please," Ares said from the bedroom.

I knew he was just trying to save me from looking at the dead woman's body, and I was thankful for the diversion. I quickly went into the kitchen and started pulling out steaks and vegetables to make for dinner. I even managed to find potatoes so I could make mashed potatoes. I kept my concentration on the meal and only when it was completed did I let myself step back and admire my work. The steaks smelled delicious, the mashed potatoes were perfectly smooth and buttery, and the vegetables were the perfect consistency, not too hard and not too soft. I grabbed plates from the cupboards and hurried to the dining room to set everything up. Ares and the others talked in the living room as I finished bringing all of the food into the dining room. I ran up the stairs and changed into sweats and a t-shirt and then called from the dining room, "Dinner's ready."

The men walked into the room, their somber faces changing instantly to smiles as they surveyed the food I'd made. Ares walked over to me, put his arm around my waist and kissed me on the lips. "It looks delicious."

I noted the hint of surprise in his voice and asked, "Did you think I didn't know how to cook?"

Ares laughed. "I was worried."

We all sat down, Ares and I at the ends of the table with

Koda, Matt and Achilles filling in between. Ares raised a hand as I started to reach for the food. I set my hand down and stared at him as he closed his eyes, bowed his head and whispered, "Thank you, Mother of All, for keeping us alive and allowing such a great meal to be prepared for us. We, as always, are in your debt. We ask only that you keep our fur clean, our teeth and claws sharp and a meal in our bellies."

I looked around the table and found everyone, including Achilles, with their heads bowed and eyes closed.

The others mumbled something and then Ares opened his eyes. "Now you may eat."

It took a moment for the shock to wear off before I started putting food on my plate. They prayed? Who was the Mother of All? Was he referring to Asena, the mother of the werewolves?

The meal was eaten in relative silence, but even with Achilles and Matt there, it was comfortable silence. As soon as I filled my stomach, I started rushing around and picking up empty plates. Ares stood up and blocked my path to the kitchen. He gently took the pile of plates out of my hands and then nodded at the other men. As one, Koda, Matt and Achilles stood and started clearing the table. Ares bumped me to the side with his hip and I stared in awe as four men, no four *warriors* did the dishes. *Where's a camera when you need one?*

As soon as the men finished the dishes, they all walked out of the house. I followed them quickly as they made their way into the woods. *Where the hell were they going?* They all stopped in the training field and turned to face me. *Uh oh.* Ares looked grim as he stood in the center of the field. "Since you insist on fighting, I thought it would be good for us to train you, all of us."

Achilles took his spot on the grass and leaned against a tree. I looked back at Ares, Koda, and Matt and felt a lump form in my throat. "I have to fight all of you?"

Matt laughed and then spoke in his British accent that I used to love, "We all specialize in different areas of fighting."

I nodded, remembering one of my kidnappers in France talking about Koda being really good at karate. "Okay."

Ares exhaled and smiled. "Okay, come attack me."

"Can I use my Sidhe powers?" I asked.

Ares shook his head. "Nope, just your wolf ones."

I didn't want to fight Ares, the idea itself was ridiculous, but the wolf side of me was excited to play fight. I let my instincts propel my movements, but kept control of my body, not letting myself change. I punched at Ares, but he dodged. I kicked, but he pushed my upper body, making me stumble. The more I tried to hit him and the more he remained untouched, the angrier I grew. Soon I stopped *trying* to hit him and let my subconscious and the wolf take over. My fist grazed Ares' cheek and a jubilant smile broke out on my face. Ares smiled back at me and began attacking, putting me on defense. His movements were too fast for me to track and soon I was surviving his blows by instinct. Matt jumped from behind me and started trying to fight me as well, causing me to move twice as fast. Then Koda jumped into the fray, kicking and punching. With the three of them attacking, I was getting hit and kicked and left with no time to think. My fists hurt from hitting them, so I changed them to paws and began clawing at the men, opening a large gash on Matt's arm. I started to get the upper hand until all three men changed their hands to paws as well.

My arms and chest stung with the numerous cuts from their claws, and I lost my endurance. Slipping in the grass, I fell to one knee and then the flame of magic inside of me flared up and covered me in a bright purple light. The men couldn't get past the barrier of purple light surrounding me and were forced to stop their attack. Ares growled at me. "I said no Sidhe powers."

Achilles spoke before I could. "She did not intentionally use them. Her body recognized it was near losing and formed the ward for her." He walked towards me and reached a hand towards my ward. Ares growled, but Achilles placed his hand on the ward anyways. His eyes widened. "This is quite impressive. Most are not able to create as seamless a ward as this." He ran his hand along the ward making the purple light pulse everywhere he touched and making my body shiver as though he were touching my skin.

I pulled at the invisible force covering me and willed it back into my body. Slowly the light ebbed and then disappeared. I collapsed onto the ground gasping for air. Achilles squatted down next to me, smiling. "You have to learn to pace yourself when it comes to magic." Achilles stood and turned to Ares. "I need to work with her on her magic. Whatever qualms you have with me and whatever disputes we have between us regarding her do not matter in this instance. If she is not taught, she may cause a catastrophic event."

Ares nodded. "I understand, but you are not allowed to touch her."

Achilles smiled smugly. "It amuses me that you think one touch from me, and she would run into my arms instead of yours."

I growled loudly at Achilles, causing Ares and him to start in surprise. "I will *never* run into your arms. I am not yours. I am tired of you tormenting Ares. Why won't you just leave us and let us be happy!" By the end I was screaming even though I had not intended to.

Achilles looked hurt as he said, "Because you will see soon enough that I offer something for you as well." He strode out of the field and into the darkening forest.

Ares helped me stand and smiled down at me. "Well, that was interesting. You fought fairly well, but your reactions are slow. We'll have to work on that."

"Can we take a shower? My body is itching with all of the cuts and the grass covering me," I said as I leaned against him. He started to pick me up, but I pushed him. "I'll run."

He didn't seem as bothered by my statement as I'd expected, but simply held my hand as we started running towards the house.

Koda and Matt were arguing about something when we finally arrived at the house. People started coming out of the surrounding houses to see what all the commotion was about.

Matt growled loudly and yelled, "I challenge Koda for place in the pack and rights as second!"

I frowned. "Rights?"

Koda snarled. "I accept!"

Ares and Achilles were on the porch of the house talking quietly, leaving me alone beside Koda and Matt. "Hey, guys, let's just calm down and—"

Matt and Koda started fighting each other, their snarls and punches almost deafening me. I started to move forward, to stop them, but Darius grabbed my arm tightly. "You cannot stop a challenge once it has been accepted."

I stared at the King of Werewolves and felt his power. He pressed it on to me, and I realized I was staring into his eyes. I looked down and nodded in understanding and acknowledgement of my submission to him. He let go of my arm, and

I moved away from him as quickly as I could without running.

Achilles moved down the steps and lifted the sleeve of my shirt to expose red marks where Darius had grabbed me. Achilles skin glowed softly as he turned to Darius. "I believe the king may have forgotten how to handle the Sidhe."

Darius frowned in confusion. "Speak freely, Achilles."

Achilles pulled me forward and lifted the sleeve of my shirt. "You've marked her skin."

Darius' eyes widened. "I did not mean to mark her. I was simply stopping her from interfering."

Ares walked down the steps and stood beside us. "Be careful, King. An offense such as this would have started wars not long ago."

Darius glared at Ares. "Perhaps you should teach your *half-breed* bitch our rules, and I would not have to touch her."

Ares growled at him, and I felt his anger and Achilles' anger rising at the same time. It was like they were feeding off of each other's emotions. Ares whispered, "You should watch your tongue, Darius. You aren't as loved as you once were."

Darius snarled. "Watch your words. There are many who do not love you as much either, Prince."

Matt screamed in pain, and I remembered why we were there. I scolded myself for being distracted and yelled, "Stop fighting! Please!" I pushed around Ares to see Matt bleeding from his arm and Koda smiling happily. "Koda, please!" I begged.

Neither seemed to hear me though, as Koda grabbed Matt around the throat and choked him. "Submit to me," Koda growled.

Matt growled and struggled against Koda, refusing to submit.

"Ares, why are they fighting?" I asked.

Achilles whispered, "If the alpha dies, the second in the pack becomes alpha and takes the previous alpha's mate."

Me. They were fighting for the right to take me if Ares ever died.

"You stupid, idiotic men. Stop fighting!" I yelled at them.

Koda punched Matt in the throat and Matt whispered, "Submit."

The crowd clapped and cheered, and Koda smiled happily. I shook my head and walked inside the house, ignoring both men. "Idiots."

For the next two days, Ares, Koda, and Matt trained with me. Soon I was able to keep pace with Matt and almost with Koda, but Ares beat me every time. I had no doubt that Natasha wasn't as skilled as Ares, so I wasn't worried.

I continued trying to half-shift, but every time I tried, I only changed into my wolf, so we gave up.

As the sun rose on the day of my challenge, I felt my nervousness. I rolled over and snuggled against Ares, who wrapped his arms around me and held me tight. "You don't have to do this. You could rescind your acceptance to fight," he whispered into my ear.

I gaped at his serious expression. He'd stay with me even if I backed out of the fight? He knew I couldn't do that and keep face with the rest of the pack. He'd lose respect as well for having a coward for a mate. "Ares, you know I can't back out."

Koda whined. "Artemis, if you want, we'll leave with you. We'll run and make up some story that will convince the others we *had* to go."

I rolled onto my back so I could meet eyes with each of them. "Stop this. I'm not going to lose. Everything will be fine."

Ares and Koda nuzzled my neck and inhaled my scent at the same time.

My heart felt as though it were tearing apart. Tears trailed down my cheeks as I imagined life without my pack. Ares kissed my cheeks and whispered in my ear, "Artemis, please reconsider. I can't bear to lose you."

"I have to, Ares." No matter how much I didn't want to lose Ares, I had to finish the fight. With my mind made up, I focused on the amount of training I'd had with them and felt sure I would win.

Ares climbed out of bed and stretched. "I'm going to make breakfast." As he walked away, I noticed the tension in his shoulders and back. Matt followed Ares out of the bedroom. It didn't escape my notice that Matt had said nothing while Koda and Ares had tried to convince me to stay safe.

Koda sat up and looked at me. "Artemis, if you think you're going to lose, you can ask for mercy, and she has to refrain from killing you."

"And then be forced to have no Ares and no pack? No, I couldn't do that. I'd rather die," I answered with conviction.

Koda hugged me against him. "I can't watch you die. If you ask for mercy, I'll leave Ares' pack and join you. I know I'm not Ares, but wouldn't it be better than being dead?"

"You'd leave Ares' pack to be my mate? To be the mate of a worthless mixed blood?"

Koda pulled away from me and smiled. "You aren't worthless, and I don't care what bloodlines you have. I love you, Artemis. You're my pack mate and nothing will change that."

I kissed his cheek and climbed out of bed, surprised by his offer. "I'll consider it if the need arises." Though, we both knew I wouldn't. I couldn't continue living if I wasn't Ares' mate. It would be like cutting out an organ.

We'd all chosen to sleep in shorts and shirts so I didn't need to change before I went downstairs in front of Achilles. Ares and Achilles both whispered in angry tones with one another when I walked into the kitchen, but I couldn't hear what they were saying.

Achilles looked at me with glistening eyes. "Good morning, Artemis."

I bowed my head towards him. "Good morning, Achilles."

Ares set a plate of bacon, eggs, and toast in front of me with a smile. I kissed his cheek and started eating. The men milled around the house in silence while I ate, a sense of doom clouding the air.

The time arrived, and we set out for the fight. The walk to the town center was filled with worry and sadness. In my mind, I was determined to win because I had finally found my pack, my family. But in my body, worry and fear resided, causing my hands to shake ever so slightly.

Ares squeezed my hand reassuringly and in an instant my worry was swept away and replaced with the knowledge that he loved me and no matter what, we'd always love each other.

Ares led us to a large grassy field where a large square had been marked out with white paint. It looked as if the entire town had turned out to watch my challenge, hundreds of people surrounding the square. Even the king and queen were sitting in chairs on the sidelines.

Koda stopped us at the sidelines and gave me a hard hug, whispering into my ear, "Remember what I told you."

Matt hugged me, too, and then both walked a ways back in the crowd. Achilles looked at me with sparkling eyes and softly glowing skin. The blue vines on his arms glittered like sapphires. "Win this battle Artemis," he said softly.

I nodded at him, and he quickly moved through the crowd. Ares rubbed his cheek against mine and inhaled my scent. Without thinking about it, I'd inhaled his scent as well and felt his unease within him. "I love you, Artemis. You'll win. I know you will."

Ares took my hand again and walked with me out to the center of the square where my opponent was waiting, bouncing on the balls of her feet and swinging her arms around. She smiled at Ares and then glared at me.

Ares raised his hand and the crowd silenced. "Today we witness a challenge between Artemis and Natasha, to the death. Winner earns the right to be mated to Ares, Prince of the Werewolves." The crowd gasped and began murmuring loudly. The queen stood up out of her chair, but the king put a hand on her arm and she sat back down. Ares raised his hand again, silencing the crowd. "No full changing will be allowed. Begin."

My skin itched, and my heartbeat tripled in pace as I watched Ares walk to the sidelines, never looking back at me. Natasha cracked her knuckles, bringing my attention to her. "Let's get this over with. I want to have your crap moved out of the room by sunset."

Her calm demeanor and cockiness made me seethe. "The only thing you'll be doing at sunset is paying the ferryman."

Her eyes widened for a moment before she recovered and charged at me. All thoughts shut off, and I went into battle mode. My wolf side took over, allowing me to use instinct to avoid most of her attacks. Unfortunately, she was faster than

I'd thought, and I was soon bleeding from my lip and a cut above my eye.

I changed tactics and instead of being defensive, I became offensive, jabbing, upper cutting and attacking as fast as I could. I knew the crowd was cheering and booing, but all I could hear was Natasha, my breathing, and the dull thud of our fists hitting each other. My thoughts flickered to Ares and Koda as I turned to dodge her fist and noticed them in the back of the crowd, encircled by men restraining them. If I lost to Natasha, I couldn't stand to see her with Ares. I couldn't bear to see Ares with *any* other woman.

Natasha growled in frustration and changed her hands into paws. She swung her right hand at my face and I barely managed to dodge backwards, her claws slicing off a piece of hair that had come out of my ponytail. She screamed with rage and charged forward, slicing first into my forearms and then into my stomach. The wounds stung worse than I could have imagined. Natasha punched me in the face, making me stumble backwards. She took advantage of my imbalance and jumped on me, pinning my arms with her knees and began pounding my face repeatedly. She snapped my right wrist making me scream and fight to stay in my human form.

I was wrong, I couldn't beat her. I should have listened to Ares, but I hadn't and now I'd lose everything. I'd lose Ares and Koda. I'd lose my pack, my family. I'd lose my life.

She growled loudly. "You're nothing, but a worthless half-breed! Your father should have killed you when you were born as he'd promised to do. You don't deserve Ares, and I'll make sure to erase every memory of you he might possess. One night with me, and he won't even remember your name." She punctuated every sentence with a blow to my head, but her words hurt me more than any physical attack could.

Anger boiled inside of me and before thoughts could form in my mind, I had exploded out from under her and grabbed Natasha, holding her up in the air by her throat. "Ares is mine," I said with conviction.

Natasha kicked and scratched at me. "Put. Me. Down."

I squeezed her throat harder. "Ares is my mate!"

I didn't want to kill her. I didn't want to kill anybody. I knew I had to end the fight, but I wanted to make her submit. As I debated what to do, she jammed her claws into my shoulder, making me drop her to the ground. I backed away from her, but she ran forward, slamming into me, sending us head over heels together.

She ended up on top of me and pinned me to the ground. "You're not meant to be the Beta's mate. You're too weak to be his."

She picked me up and threw me across the square. I landed on my face and felt a rib crack. She was on me again before I could roll over. She grabbed me by the hair and stood me up before kicking me in the side. The force of her kick knocked the wind out of me and broke another rib. She squatted down next to me as I gasped for air and writhed in the grass. "It's time to end this. It's time to finish you and take you out of Ares' life once and for all."

She turned my head, and I found Ares at the edge of the square being held back by four men. His eyes glowed golden as he looked at me. Koda and Achilles were near Ares, but both of them were also being held back by people. I reached out to them and brushed their wolves' energies with mine. My energy was depleted and it was only a matter of minutes before I died, whether by Natasha or the internal bleeding I could sense.

"I love you," I whispered. Tears leaked out of my eyes as I looked at the man I loved and my pack mate.

Ares growled angrily and struggled against the men holding him. "Artemis. No!" More men surrounded Ares and Koda.

Natasha turned my face back and smiled. "What a sweet goodbye." Her claws pierced my stomach as she drove them deep into my body.

I screamed and thrashed against her, pulling her hand out of me and smashing her nose with my fist. She stumbled backwards, eyes wide, and I pounced on her. I couldn't lose Ares. I couldn't die. Dammit, I couldn't lose.

In a matter of seconds, I had my arm around her throat and my legs around her waist with my left hand pushing her neck deeper into my arm. "Ask for mercy," I whispered.

She nodded once, and I released her, collapsing on the ground myself. I rolled onto my back and exhaled.

I'd won, but I could feel my life ending. *At least I'd won.* Natasha roared and jumped at me. I lifted my hand up, summoning what little energy I had left, and my Sidhe powers. A small fireball sped from my hand to her and disappeared through her chest. She staggered for a minute, looking down at the hole in her chest, before collapsing to the ground. Her lifeless body lay next to me, and I knew it was right that I'd won.

I took one more breath, whispered, "I love you, Ares," and then darkness consumed me.

THE AFTERLIFE WASN'T what I'd expected. First, I hadn't expected to be woken in the afterlife by a slap in the face. And second, I didn't expect to find Ares and Achilles sitting next to me.

"Artemis! Artemis, wake up!" Ares yelled at me.

"You're not dead. How can you be here?" I asked.

"Artemis, you're not dead," Achilles said through clenched teeth.

"My energy. It was drained," I said completely confused.

Ares put my hand against his face. "Yes, but Achilles and I have been loaning you ours."

The woozy feeling in my head disappeared, and I could feel my body. Everything hurt. Gwen, the healer, knelt beside me. "Artemis, where does it hurt?"

"Everywhere," I groaned.

She ran her hands along my body and then cursed softly. "Ares, how much of your energy are you willing to give up?"

Ares continued to stare at my face as he spoke. "I'll give everything."

She stared at him for a moment before shaking her head. "I won't kill you to save her, but that won't be necessary anyways because I'm sure the Sidhe Prince will loan me some of his energy as well, since he's already doing it."

Achilles nodded. "You can use as much as you need."

She looked quizzically at Achilles as he stared at me. It unnerved me to see the same look on Achilles' face that Ares' had on his. She studied the two men a minute longer and then shrugged. "Alright. Let's get started."

In ten minutes, she'd healed all of my wounds, including the internal bleeding and broken ribs. Her body slumped forward and her face looked gray as she finished. "She won't have enough energy to do more than rest in bed for the next few days. Keep her lying down as much as you can."

Ares picked me up and cradled me against his chest. "Thank you."

Ares turned around and I saw Koda unconscious on the ground. "Ares, what happened to Koda?" I asked with wide eyes.

Ares sighed. "You stopped breathing for a minute and he went ballistic, flinging the men around him away and trying to rush to you. I'd already gotten to you though, and he was so upset that he had started to change. Darius knocked him out. He'll be fine."

Matt walked over and smiled at me. "Hey, Love. Glad to see you're doing better." He picked Koda up and started walking back towards the house.

Ares followed him, nuzzling my cheek with his nose every few steps. Even though my body was healed, Gwen had been right, I felt exhausted.

I closed my eyes as I relaxed in Ares' hold. I felt safe and protected with his arms around me. Just as I started to doze off, I realized that I'd won. I'd beat Natasha and kept Ares as my mate. I'd actually won. Ares hummed softly and despite my attempts not to, I fell into a deep sleep.

THREE DAYS of bed rest was causing me to go insane. Ares wouldn't even let me walk down the stairs. If I started towards the stairs, he would pick me up and carry me down them, despite my protests.

My strength was finally back to normal as I sat in front of Ares and Koda, trying to convince them to go on a hunt. "Ares, come on. I need to get out of the house and I really want to do something as a pack."

Ares folded his arms across his chest and answered without hesitation. "No."

Koda frowned at me. "You *died* three days ago."

"I didn't die three days ago. I *almost* died."

Koda folded his arms across his chest. "*You* died. Achilles' and Ares' energies and magic were the only ones present in your body."

I sprang to my feet and stormed toward the front door. Achilles suddenly blocked my path. "Artemis, be reasonable." Ever since he'd donated his energy to save me, I'd felt a strange connection to him.

"You be reasonable. I *need* to go outside!" I yelled up at Achilles, not caring that he was a prince or that I shouldn't be yelling.

Koda walked out the front door, his shoulders stiff with anger.

Ares pulled me backwards and wrapped his arms around me. "We need to leave."

I pulled back from him to see his face. He looked tired and sad. "What? Why would we leave? Where would we go?" I asked.

Achilles cleared his throat. "Perhaps we could take her to my father's kingdom."

Ares growled softly. "No."

Achilles folded his arms over his chest. "She needs training anyways."

Koda ran inside panting. "Ares, we need to leave."

Ares looked at me with an I-told-you-so face and then turned to Koda. "Why?"

Koda exhaled. "Dhampirs, vampires, and ogres have surrounded the castle and are demanding Artemis."

Ares growled loudly and lifted his lip in a snarl. Achilles

turned to Ares. "Let me fly her out of here while you deal with the intruders. You know I can keep her safe."

Ares shook his head still snarling. "No."

Achilles and Ares began arguing loudly with each other. Slowly, I backed away from them. Ares stopped talking and turned towards me. "Where are you going?"

"The bathroom."

His eyes narrowed, but Achilles said, "She would be perfectly safe in the Sidhe realm," and Ares attention was once again off of me.

I hurried to the bathroom and stared at my reflection. Every time I looked at myself, I could barely recognize the person staring back at me. I no longer looked like a teenage girl, but now looked like a woman. It hadn't been that long, but my features were noticeably different. Could it be from gaining my Sidhe powers? Or was it from the connection with Ares and all of the drama I'd been dealing with? Whatever it was, I was no longer a child. I'd killed people, and I was stronger than a human. I was strong enough to fight my own battles. "That's it," I whispered. My skin began glowing softly, and I knew what I had to do.

Quickly and quietly I moved from the bathroom, down the hallway and through the kitchen to the back door. Ares, Achilles and Koda were all arguing and yelling, so none of them heard me leave. I shut the door as quietly as I could and headed through town. Everyone stared at me as I walked by, but no one tried to stop me. Energy flowed through me and for the first time I felt the energy of the plants around me. Every living thing was filled with energy. Could I use that energy somehow?

A group of twenty people stood on the edge of the village at the beginning of the forest, while another group of twenty werewolves stood at the edge of the village facing them. Half of the werewolves present were in wolf form, so I knew I had to hurry because they would communicate to Ares telepathically that I was here without him.

I stepped just past the line of werewolves to stand alone between the two groups. The werewolves began murmuring, and the dhampirs and vampires in front of me simply smiled. My skin was still glowing softly, and it gave me hope that this would work. I squared my shoulders and spoke as loudly and as strongly as I could, "You are trespassing. Please leave the premises."

The dhampirs and vampires looked at each other for a moment before one of them walked forward. He was a short man, thin and unimposing, yet I could feel the evil radiating off of him in waves. How can you tell the difference between a vampire and a dhampir? Two ways. One, dhampirs are more muscular, not bulky like the werewolves, but not thin-built like the vampires either, an in-between of the two. And two, vampires ooze evil mojo whereas dhampirs only emit a creepy level of evil. He stopped several yards away from me and bowed elegantly. "Greetings, Artemis. I am Roger. It is a pleasure to meet you." He spoke with a slight English accent that would have made me smile if I hadn't been able to feel how evil he was.

"Who sent you here?" I asked.

He smiled. "If you would please come with us, we will take you to the one requesting your presence."

He was trying to be sweet, but nothing as evil as he was could be truly sweet. My skin began glowing brighter and my powers formed a shield around me as my fear of him grew. Any vampire who was so calm when faced with a group of werewolves had to be powerful. "I am not going anywhere with you. Leave this place or die."

The werewolves behind me began murmuring excitedly.

Roger's smile widened. "You think you can take us all on?"

I clenched and unclenched my hands and visualized fire covering them. Instantly, my visualization came true. Purple flames flickered around my hands as I smiled at Roger. "I can try."

One of the dhampirs yelled and began running towards me. I held up my hand, palm facing the dhampir and a fireball flew from my hand and through the dhampir's chest. The body fell to the ground and the rest of the vampires and dhampirs began rushing towards me. I backed up as I continued to send fireball after fireball into the group.

The werewolves behind me finally regained their composure and rushed forward to join the fight. I dropped my shield to conserve energy while I continued firing at my enemies. Roger dodged three of my fireballs and punched me in the face, making the flames around my hands disappear, and I stumbled backwards. His fists flew too fast for me to track and soon I was bleeding, in pain, and on my back on the ground. He jumped at me, and I flipped him over my body using my legs. I was up and fighting with another vampire before his body had even hit the dirt. More dhampirs and vampires poured into the area, easily outnumbering us.

I had been wrong. I couldn't take on this many. I could barely handle twenty. "ARES!" I yelled as loudly as I could. The connection between us would have notified him immediately when I was in pain so I knew he had to feel the fear I felt. "ARES!" I yelled one more time before Roger tackled me from behind while I was exchanging blows with a dhampir.

I grunted from the impact and tried to roll over, but

Roger's fingers turned to claws, and he stabbed me in the side, holding me in place. "The boss didn't say you couldn't be hurt, just that you couldn't be dead. I have a lot of leeway between living and dead."

His arrogant attitude angered me more than the fact that he wanted to torture me. I grabbed his hand at the wrist and pulled his claws from my side. My skin began glowing and I smiled up at him. "It's going to make your boss really unhappy when he learns that you failed."

Roger tried to pry his wrist free from my hand, but I held tight and then faster than I'd ever been able to summon it before, flame covered my hand and instantly ate through his wrist, bone and all. I tossed his severed hand aside and plunged my hand into his chest like I'd done with the female vampire who'd tried to kill me. He began screaming and I quickly pulled his heart from his chest and turned it to ash. I pushed him off of me and stood up, the flames leaving my hand. Everyone was staring at me and the screaming vampire with a hole in his chest.

I felt Ares nearby, but didn't look at him as I walked around to Roger's head and picked him up by the back of his neck with his screaming head facing towards the other vampires and dhampirs.

"I asked you to leave. I even said 'please', but you still stayed to try to capture me. I am not as easy a prey as you were told." I had to shout to be heard over Rogers' screams. "You will find that my compassion only goes so far." The flames covered my hands again, and I placed them around Roger's neck. His screams intensified as the flames began covering his body. Apparently, vampires do burn easily by fire. Score one for Hollywood on that truth.

I dropped Roger's body to the ground as he burned and

screamed, though his screams only lasted twenty more seconds because Achilles stepped forward and decapitated him with a sword.

The other vampires and dhampirs stood still in shock for a moment, staring at Roger's body before their eyes raised and they looked at me. As one, they screamed their rage and rushed towards me. Achilles sword flashed several times, decapitating those nearest me. Ares came to stand next to me in half-shift. I extinguished the flames covering my hands and set my hand against Ares' forearm, letting our bond heal the wounds on my body. He looked down at me, and his lips pulled up in what I guessed to be a smile. The smile only lasted a minute though because I'd angered the vampires and dhampirs more than I'd scared them, and they were coming towards me fast. Ares moved with deadly precision, killing one after another after another. I watched him in awe.

Achilles sword slashed down just to the right of me and I blinked at the severed arm that fell beside my body. Achilles decapitated the owner of the arm and then held his hand out to me. "Come, we must get you far away from here."

I looked towards Ares who was fighting with two vampires at once. "I can't."

Achilles groaned in frustration and picked me up in his arms. "He will get over me touching you as long as you're safe."

I looked around us and realized that we were vastly outnumbered as more dhampirs and vampires and even a group of ogres joined the fight from the depths of the forest. Achilles' body glowed and the blue vines on his upper chest and arms throbbed in time with his heart and then wings spread from his back. His wings matched the color of the vines on his skin. They were one of the most beautiful things I'd ever seen.

"Where did your sword go?" I asked curiously.

Achilles smiled down at me, making my breath catch in my throat. "Perhaps now is not the time to discuss that?"

I looked at the fighting going on and blushed in embarrassment. "Right." It wasn't my fault that I was easily distracted.

Achilles wings moved and we were suddenly above the fight. "Ares!" Achilles called. Ares looked up and growled loudly. "I'm taking her to safety. Meet us in your meadow."

Ares roared in anger and began attacking more fiercely, killing four vampires and two dhampirs in a matter of seconds.

Achilles moved his wings, and we were up above the trees and the people below looked like small ants. I wrapped my arms around Achilles' neck and trembled.

"What's wrong?" Achilles asked softly.

I closed my eyes and put my face against his neck. "I hate heights."

Achilles laughed, shaking his chest and me against it. "A fairy afraid of heights? Now that is original."

I pulled back to glare at him, but instead, found myself staring at the trees zooming past us like green blurs. We were flying incredibly fast and yet I felt no wind pressing against me. I looked up and noticed the slight blue tinge of a shield around us. "Why do you have a shield around us?"

"I thought it might frighten you more if you felt the wind while we flew."

"Oh." He was right. I probably would have been more scared. I took a deep breath and inhaled his scent. Instantly I relaxed and felt safe.

My grip loosened from his neck and Achilles smiled at me. "See, it's not so bad."

I refused to look down again. "It's not the fact that we're high up, it's the fear of falling down."

His smile disappeared as he grew serious. "Do you think I would drop you?"

I pulled my gaze from his lips up to his eyes. "I don't know. I hardly know you."

"Whose fault is that?" he asked sadly.

I looked over his face as I tried to gauge what mood he was in. He was mad, sad and yet seemed happy all at the same time. "Why didn't you come to me before?" I asked.

Achilles frowned a moment before sighing. "Your father forbade me from visiting you. I didn't understand why before, but now that I know he hadn't told you what you really are, it makes perfect sense. If you had seen me, then you would know that you aren't human and he wanted you to think you were human for as long as he could."

My heart was beating faster than normal as we flew farther and farther away from Ares. My skin started itching and my breath came in short pants. Achilles' wings stilled and we began falling down towards the ground. I grabbed on to his neck and closed my eyes as we fell. I knew that he wouldn't hurt himself and that I shouldn't be worried, but I couldn't control my emotions very well with Ares so far away.

Achilles was suddenly walking, and I realized we'd landed. I opened my eyes and looked at the beautiful meadow we were in. Wild flowers filled most of the meadow and added amazingly bright purples, pinks, reds and blues to the area.

Achilles walked towards an area with tree trunks set around a circle of rocks where a camp fire could be started. Achilles laid me down in the grass and wild flowers and looked up at the moon. My breathing had leveled out, but my heart was still beating fast and my skin still tingled. Could that mean Ares was closer? I sat up and looked at Achilles who was sitting on a log and starting a fire using his Sidhe powers. "Did you call this Ares' meadow?"

Achilles moved the pieces of wood in the fire around before turning to me. "Yes. We're actually halfway between the werewolves and the Sidhe and this is Ares' land. This spot was his favorite to go to for meditations as I recall."

I approached Achilles with a purple wild flower in my hand. "You know Ares very well, don't you?"

Achilles poked at the fire with a stick. "Yes."

I sat on the log beside him. "What is he hiding from me? He hasn't told me anything about his past. I can only get bits and pieces from him."

Achilles tossed the stick into the fire and shook his head. "I cannot tell you. If he's withholding the information from you, then he must have a reason. I have no idea what the reason could be, but nevertheless he must have one."

I looked at the vines on his arms and watched as they throbbed. I lifted my finger and ran the tip of it down one of his vines. The vine sparkled brighter and then every vine on his body glowed brightly, and his skin exploded in white light. Achilles gasped and then groaned.

I yanked my hand back and moved away from him. I hadn't meant to hurt him. I'd just been mesmerized by the vines.

Achilles looked up at me, his eyes completely white, like two glowing pearls. "Don't be afraid," he said softly. I relaxed and he smiled. "Do you know what you just did?" Before I could answer, he shook his head and laughed. "Of course, you don't. You don't know anything of our kind." He shook his head sadly for a moment and then looked up at me again, a look of pure joy on his face. "You just released my powers with a single touch. It's rare because the one that can do that, is your destined mate."

I shook my head and backed up until the backs of my legs hit another log. "No. I can't be your destined mate if I'm Ares'."

Achilles gestured at his glowing body. "The results do not lie. You are my destined mate." He sighed, sounding exhausted, and his body stopped glowing. His eyes returned to normal and he shook his head sadly. "It's going to take years to come to an agreement with Ares."

I realized that my skin wasn't tingly anymore and my heartbeat was almost normal. "He's close by," I said.

Achilles frowned. "Hm."

I sat down beside him and sighed. "Can you wait to tell Ares about what happened? I'd rather deal with him being mad at me for trying to fight the vampires first instead of him being mad at me for touching you as well."

Achilles huffed a laugh. "I think you're right."

We sat in comfortable silence for an hour before I felt Ares approaching. I walked out of the ring of logs and towards the direction he was coming from. My heart beat faster each time I turned in the right direction, like a homing beacon.

Ares, Koda, and Matt finally came into view, and I exhaled happily. Ares sped up, running ahead of the others and picked me up in his arms, swinging me around a couple times before setting me back down on my feet. "Artemis, you're alright."

I kissed his face and lips several times before I looked into his eyes. "Of course I'm alright."

Ares kissed me roughly on the lips and hugged me tightly again. "Don't you ever try to fight without me again."

I nuzzled my nose into his neck and whined happily. "I'm sorry."

Koda and Matt finally arrived, and Ares released me so that I could hug each of them and rub noses to inhale each other's scents.

Ares picked up my hand and walked the rest of the way to the camp fire. "Thank you for protecting her," he said softly.

Achilles bowed his head. "Anytime, Brother."

Brother?

Ares growled. "We are not brothers."

Achilles sighed and poked at the fire with a new stick. Matt and Koda worked together and hung skinned rabbits and a skinned fox over the fire to cook. Looking at the cooking animals made me realize how thirsty I was. I stripped from my clothes, setting them on the log beside Ares and changed to my wolf form. I stretched and shook after the shift and then trotted over to the small stream I'd heard on the other side of the meadow. The men watched me until I started drinking from the stream and then turned back around and began talking.

After I had my fill of water, I jogged over to the logs, changed forms again and pulled my clothes on. It felt good and right to change forms now. I wish I'd known about it sooner so that I could have enjoyed it more.

I sat down beside Ares and rested my head against his shoulder. He was involved in a serious debate with Achilles, but he pulled me in against him so that his arms were around my shoulders while his thumb lightly stroked my skin. I tried to pay attention to what they were discussing, but I felt a presence out in the dark of the night. It was as if I was being poked in the stomach. I stood, and Ares grabbed my hand. I turned to look at him and saw his mouth moving, but I couldn't hear anything. I put my hands to my ears and then shook my head. Ares' and Achilles' mouths moved quickly and Koda and Matt ran off into the night. The poking in my stomach grew stronger until it felt as though something had pierced my skin. I screamed in pain and fell to the ground as I felt my energy being drained.

I couldn't see my attacker. I didn't even know *what* my attacker was. How could I fight it?

Ares had his hands resting against my face as he talked to me, but I couldn't hear his words. Tears streamed down my face as the unseen attacker continued to drain me. What could be so powerful that it could kill you without ever even touching you?

Achilles pushed Ares aside and grabbed me in his arms. His wings sprung from his back and then we were up in the air. I hung limp in his arms as he flew. Achilles' mouth was moving fast and then he pressed his forehead to mine. Images and thoughts filled my mind and I realized after a few moments that they were Achilles' memories. I gasped and then the images and thoughts stopped, denying me the chance to make sense of what I'd seen.

Are you alright?

I gasped again as the question was spoken in Achilles' voice, but through my mind. "How can I hear you in my head?"

Achilles shook his head and I saw his chest heave as he sighed. *It would be best if you didn't speak out loud.*

"Is this like the werewolves' communication while in wolf form?" I asked out loud.

Yes. Now please stop talking out loud.

Sorry. Why can I hear you in my head anyways?

We'll discuss that later. For now, we must discuss what

happened. You were attacked by the Queen of the Light Court, Hera—

Wait...isn't the queen your mom?

Yes, but...

Why did your mom attack me?

She was simply testing your powers first, which is why I didn't interfere, but when she realized that you are more powerful than her, she grew angry and tried to kill...

I'm more powerful than her? How is that possible? Does that mean that I—

Stop interrupting me! Listen to me, Artemis. We don't have much time. She's following us. I'm going to take you to my father's kingdom because he will protect you. My mother and he have been fighting for decades, and she's not allowed to enter his kingdom. It's the safest place for you. Ares will meet us soon.

Why is she following us?

She wants you dead. She's very jealous and has always tried to kill those more powerful than her. Vanity is one of her negative qualities that have caused many wars over the centuries.

Achilles landed on top of a hill covered in bright green grass beside the ocean and set me down on my feet.

Where are we?

Ireland.

How did we get here so fast?

Achilles rolled his eyes at me. *We're not as slow as birds or airplanes. We're preternaturals, which means we have extraordinary powers. Powers great enough to fly across the world in an hour.* He walked down the hill a little way and stopped in front of a square patch of dead grass. He placed his hand against the patch of grass and then his skin began to glow. The dead grass dropped down and the hole widened until it was at least ten feet by ten feet and a set of stairs was visible leading into the ground. Achilles picked up my hand and started walking down the stairs. I followed him down and swallowed nervously as the top shrank and the grass returned to cover the hole behind us. We continued down the steps in complete darkness.

CHAPTER

SEVEN

We descended the stairs in complete darkness and I felt my nerves increasing.

Achilles?

Yes?

I know it's childish, but could you maybe... Before I could finish my thought, Achilles' skin began glowing and Lit the area around us. We were surrounded by stone instead of dirt and we walked down a narrow stairway that seemed to never end. I gripped Achilles' hand tighter as I began to feel claustrophobic. The wolf didn't like feeling trapped and deep underneath a hill in a stone stairway, close enough to a cage for us as a real one.

Achilles spun around suddenly and put his hands on each side of my face and stared into my eyes. *Easy. We're going to be fine. The door is just ahead and through that we enter into my father's realm. It's completely open. You're not trapped. This is not a cage—simply a passageway. You can't change.*

His touch and words relaxed me until I could breathe normally again. He turned back around and walked faster.

Why had his touch relaxed me? Only Ares should have been able to do that? Did it have something to do with his new ability to communicate telepathically with me? Did he do something? Or was he right about the destined mate thing?

I was trying to figure out an answer when he pushed open a door and sunlight temporarily blinded me. Achilles continued to pull me forward as my eyes adjusted. I tugged on his hand to stop him and rubbed my eyes with my palms. I slowly opened my eyes, and then my mouth dropped open.

In books, the fairy realm was simply an underground castle or a large underground room. They were completely wrong. It wasn't an underground anything. Birds flew in the blue skies above us and the oceans splashed against the cliffs nearby. I turned around and instead of seeing the door we'd come through I saw even more beautiful grassy land.

How?

The Sidhe do not live in the underground as humans like to believe. We live in a different dimension, which you can get to by using a portal, such as the one we used to get here.

A different dimension? That's crazy.

Crazy, but true. Come, we must hurry.

Achilles picked my hand up again and led me towards a giant stone castle. We had to walk through a village, and I stared in awe at the people dressed in fine clothes. *Why are they dressed as though they live in the medieval era?*

Achilles continued walking as he talked to me. *The medieval era is my father's favorite, so those that live in the Dark Court wear that period of clothing and even speak as they would during that time period. My father is somewhat egotistical, as you can imagine.*

The people all wore medieval clothing yet their skin was of every color of the rainbow with various designs on their skins. Some had their wings out, but most had their wings hidden. Men, women and children stared at us as we walked. Achilles seemed to ignore the looks while I couldn't help but look back. Were they staring at Achilles or me?

We made it to the castle and Achilles smiled. "Morning, guards."

The two guards, dressed in full armor, pushed open the doors and bowed their heads. "Greetings, Prince Achilles."

We started to walk past them when I caught their scent. I stopped walking and stared at them in shock. "Werewolves?"

I realized my hearing returned, and would have been excited if the two guards hadn't started sniffing at me. One of them reached out towards me, and I growled at him, snapping my teeth. He pulled his hand back and gaped at me. "Who are you?"

I opened my mouth to answer when a tall man with a long white beard stepped through the doors to stand beside Achilles. "She is Artemis, daughter of Darren of the Werewolves and Athena of the Sidhe, and fiancée of Prince Achilles of the Sidhe."

The man looked like Achilles, except he was slightly older and had a long white beard. I knew who he was instantly. I curtsied and bowed my head. "Greetings Zeus, King of the Dark Court of the Sidhe."

Zeus laughed happily. "I see you've started training her."

Achilles sighed. "We must speak father. It's important."

Zeus picked my hand up, and I straightened to look at him. He kissed the back of my hand and smiled seductively at me. "It's nice to finally meet you."

A blush instantly covered my cheeks, but I found my voice and said, "It's an honor to finally meet you."

Zeus took my hand and placed it on the inside of his

elbow as he led us into the castle. The hallways were wide enough to ride three horses abreast and torches sat in decorative iron holders every five feet or so. Achilles walked on the other side of me as we made our way past large rooms filled with Sidhe of every color. I tried to stop to look, but Zeus continued to pull me along. He stopped in front of a set of large, ornately carved wooden doors and snapped his fingers. The two guards in front of the doors pushed them open and then stepped out of the way as Zeus led me inside.

The king's bedroom is expected to be elegant, but the King of the Sidhe's bedroom was magnificent. He kept to his medieval time period though, not having a single modern item inside. Zeus released my hand, and I walked quickly to the balcony, pushing aside the red drapes to look out over the ocean below.

The wind whipped against my face, sending a light spray of water to chill me. I'd never seen anything so beautiful. I looked up and felt the sun's rays heat my face. Everything felt so real, yet how could this exist without the humans knowing about it?

Achilles walked to stand on the balcony beside me and leaned his elbows on the stone railing. "This is my favorite spot in all of the Dark Court."

"I can see why," I said softly as I looked out over the ocean. A whale breached the waves a mile or so away from us and sprayed water up into the air.

Achilles picked my hand up and turned me to face him. "Your eyes are glowing with energy. You're even more beautiful when standing beside the ocean."

The wind whipped my hair from side to side as Achilles and I stared at each other. The desire to kiss him was almost as bad as it had been with Ares, but thinking of Ares helped cool my hormones and allow me to turn away from him. "Thank you."

A table had been set up in Zeus' bedroom while I'd been on the balcony. I hurried inside and sat down in a chair and began piling meat and cheese on to my plate.

"So, what brings you here?" Zeus asked Achilles.

Achilles sat down beside me and nibbled on some fruits and cheeses as he spoke. "Let's see, where to begin? Well, first let me tell you that Mother attacked Artemis and wishes to kill her..."

Zeus stood up and stared at Achilles. "Is that why you..."

Achilles held up his hand. "Yes, I only did it out of necessity."

"Did what out of necessity, my dear son?" asked a woman.

Achilles was instantly out of his chair and standing beside me, his skin glowing.

The woman was beyond beautiful. Her skin was like buttery cream with a beautiful filigree design which glowed as she looked at me and Achilles. "You had better explain why you are assuming an attack stance against me."

Achilles spoke softly. "She's my fiancée, Mother. I will not let you hurt her."

Hera looked at me with clear disdain. I met her eyes as I continued to eat. If she wanted to kill me, she probably could, so I would at least die with a full stomach.

I won't let her kill you.

My eyes flickered over to Achilles as he spoke to me, but I quickly looked back at Hera. *Can't she technically order you to kill me if she wanted to?*

Yes, but she won't do that because...

"Are you communicating telepathically?" she hissed.

Achilles glared at her. "You tried to kill her! What else could I do?"

"*You. Bound. Her?*" She asked in angry pants. Her skin began glowing again, and her eyes turned to white pearls as Achilles' had done when I'd released his powers.

Bound me? What did that mean?

"There was no other way. I had to save her," Achilles said through clenched teeth.

Hera stopped glowing and turned away. "You were always an impulsive man."

I turned to Zeus, since he wasn't involved in their conversation either. I might as well get as much information from them as possible while I was here. Who knew when the next time I'd be allowed to go to the Sidhe court would be? "Do all Sidhe have Greek names?" I asked.

Zeus smiled. "Technically we had the names first, but the humans used to believe that we were gods and so their stories were based on us."

I looked from Zeus to Hera and then back to Zeus. "Is she really your sister?"

Hera gasped, and Zeus laughed. "No. Most of the family trees that the humans created are wrong. Hera is not my sister, only my wife."

"So, can you really use lightning bolts?" I asked curiously.

Zeus put his arm out, palm up. His skin started glowing and then a sizzling lightning bolt appeared in his hand. "Some of what the humans recorded about us is true," he said.

"Wow." I chewed on a grape when it occurred to me that "Ares" was a Greek name, too. "Wait. Are the Sidhe who the humans based their stories off of the only ones with Greek mythological names?"

Achilles opened his mouth to say something, but Zeus said, "Yes."

I stood up from my chair and walked quickly towards the balcony. *That was it. That was what Ares had been keeping from me. He is part Sidhe, too.*

Achilles stood next to me and put a hand on my back. "I cannot tell you his story. It's very personal, and I feel it is best for him to tell you himself."

"Who are you talking about?" Hera asked, narrowing her eyes at us. "I hate it when I'm out of the loop."

Achilles turned around. "Why is she here? In your realm?" he asked Zeus.

I turned around and found Hera sitting on Zeus' lap. Zeus sighed, "Well, son, you see…"

Achilles groaned. "You're dating again! You remember what happened last time?"

Hera shrugged. "It was a small battle."

Achilles scoffed. "A small battle? You call *World War Two* a small battle?"

Zeus turned to me and asked, "Do you have wings?"

I shrugged. "I'm not sure. I didn't know you had wings until Achilles showed me, and I haven't tried to get them out."

Zeus stood up out of his chair, helped Hera sit down in it, then walked to me and took my hand. "Focus on your surroundings. Do you feel the energy from all of the living things around you?"

I nodded.

"Good, now focus on those energies and ask them to loan you some of their strength."

If my life hadn't been as crazy as it was, I would have thought he was joking with me or that he was insane. Instead I closed my eyes and asked the plants to borrow some of their energy. I opened my eyes when I felt the excess energy flowing through me and lighting my body up like a fluorescent light bulb.

Zeus smiled. "Good. Now close your eyes and picture your back. In the center of your back between your shoulder blades I want you to picture two vertical slits, one foot long each."

I pictured exactly what he said and then felt my skin rip apart and my wings flare out behind me. The pain forced me to my knees, and my body sizzled as though I'd been electrocuted. Zeus helped me stand up and walked around me to look at my wings and body. "Interesting," he said as he came back to face me.

"How do I move them?" I asked after the pain had subsided.

Achilles smiled from beside me. "You just think what you want and they do it. Once you get used to it they move like your arms or legs, almost without thought."

I moved my right wing forward and stared at the purple wings with purple vines. "Purple vines?"

Zeus whispered, "They match your eyes, your new skin marks and the streaks in your hair."

"Streaks? Skin marks?" I started trying to pull my hair forward, but Achilles grabbed my wrists and then Hera snapped her fingers and a full length mirror stood before me. My black hair was now randomly streaked with purple. It was very punk and yet I loved it. My skin was a lighter color and I had thin purple lines, like flower vines covering my arms and face and as much of my body as I could see. I loved it. I looked tough and beautiful at the same time. I looked hot! But...what would Ares think? Would he still think I was beautiful?

Of course, he will.

I looked at Achilles and smiled. "Thanks."

He smiled back. *Anytime.*

Zeus cleared his throat. "Okay, now to put them away you simply imagine your back, flat and devoid of any slits or wings."

I closed my eyes and the wings disappeared. My shirt flapped forward and I clutched it to the front of me. "Great, another way to ruin clothes."

Achilles laughed. "It's alright. I'm sure we have some clothes that'll fit."

Zeus disappeared through a side door and then came back out with a large t-shirt. "It's a little big for you, but it'll work for now."

I pulled the shirt on and smiled gratefully. "Thank you."

Achilles asked, "Would you like to explore?"

I nodded vigorously. "Yes, please."

Achilles took my hand and led me out to the balcony. His wings popped out of his back, and then we were up in the air. He made his way beside the water and then to the village we'd originally walked through. He set me down on my feet and then took my hand in his and led me through the town.

I stopped at a booth where a red and blue colored Sidhe woman was selling strange looking items. Achilles started steering me away then whispered, "They're magical items that you have no need for."

I rolled my eyes. "Why do men hate shopping so much?"

He continued leading me through the town and then out into the green fields surrounding the castle area.

I relaxed and asked the question I'd been dying to know the answer to, "So, were you really the hero of the Trojan war?"

Achilles rolled his eyes. "Yes, I was the one who thought of the Horse, but I've won many other wars besides that. Unfortunately, Ares was with me and as the 'God of War' they gave him more credit than they gave me."

"So, you two used to be close then?"

Achilles sighed longingly. "It was a long time ago though."

"So, why the 'Achilles Heel'?" I asked, having been curious about that as well.

Achilles laughed. "If I had a dollar for every time someone has asked me that, I would be able to buy the world."

I stayed quiet and waited for him to explain.

"Well, as you can imagine, a hit to my heel won't kill me, but during the Trojan War I was in a terrific fight. I'd been shot by arrows and one of the Trojans was exchanging blows with me. I was growing weaker as the metal in the arrows stayed buried in my skin and then just as I was attempting to use a large portion of my magic some bastard shot me in the heel with an arrow. I screamed in pain and then my Mother appeared and, using her ability to teleport, took me to safety. Unfortunately, all the humans saw was me get shot in the heel by an arrow and then disappear in a flash of light. Can you believe that they all thought I exploded? Simply ridiculous!"

I laughed and then quickly tried to stifle it. "Sorry, I didn't mean to laugh..."

He put his hands on his hips and said, "Really? You didn't mean to..." and then he tackled me to the ground, tickling me in every ticklish spot I had.

I was laughing and struggling against him, but he seemed to be an expert at tickle torturing. I finally had to concede and yelled, "I surrender!"

He collapsed onto the ground beside me and laughed. "I haven't had that much fun in a while."

I sighed and sat up. "Me neither."

He sat up beside me and pushed my hair behind my ear. "You have fun with Ares."

I nodded. "Yes, sometimes, but the fun times are always clouded over by the awful times."

Achilles smiled. "You'll have good times with him again. He's a lot of fun to be around when he's not trying to win wars or conquer the human world."

We sat in comfortable silence for a few minutes and then Achilles asked, "Has Ares told you where each of the main races come from?"

I shook my head.

Achilles twirled a blade of grass between his fingers as he spoke. "We are children of this world, though from different parts. For instance, the werewolves are Children of the Moon, which is why your power to change comes from the moon. Humans are Children of the Sun, though their species has a strange desire to forget their histories instead of remembering, and I'm sure none of them understand that. We, Sidhe, are Children of the Stars."

He paused, and I asked, "What about vampires?"

He tore the blade of grass in his hand into two and whispered, "Vampires are Children of the Darkness, which is why the sun harms them and they are so powerful at night."

"So, I'm half star and half moon?"

Achilles nodded. "Yes."

"Which is why I'm so powerful?"

"Which is why you have the potential to become extremely powerful. You are powerful, Artemis, but you are not able to harness your power like Hera or Maurice, who are thousands of years older than you. Though, with practice and time you will become more powerful than they."

"Which is why they want me dead?"

Achilles didn't respond, but I knew the answer. Now, it made more sense. With the combined power of two dominant races I had the ability to surpass any being who was a pure-bred of any one race.

We walked back to the castle and then out to the balcony. I asked, "Can I see my mother?"

Achilles smiled. "Of course, but she lives in the Light Court, so we'll have to wait…"

Hera stood and smoothed her dress. "Nonsense. We can be there in an instant."

Achilles rubbed his temples with his fingers. "Mother, please."

Hera smiled. "You have no need to worry now, dear. Achilles has seen fit to save you from any desire I might have had about killing you."

Zeus waved at me. "Goodbye, dear. It was nice to meet you."

Achilles walked to Zeus and quickly spoke in his ear before hurrying over and grabbing my hand. Hera grabbed each of our free hands and whispered, "This might make you a little queasy," and then we were in a black spinning vortex. At least, that's what it felt like to me. When everything stopped spinning, I dropped to the ground and tried my best not to throw up.

Achilles whispered, "You'll be alright in a moment."

"Guards! Take Achilles and Artemis to their chambers. Someone else go find Athena and ask her to report to the Prince's chambers."

I looked up and stared at the men standing in the hallway. Each of them was a different color and each had various patterns and designs on their bodies. Achilles helped me stand and then an attractive, white-skinned man with exquisite black scrolling designs stepped forward. "Greetings, Artemis. I'm Erebus."

Erebus, God of Darkness and Shadow. I was actually meeting *the* Erebus. How cool was that?

"It's an honor to meet you, Erebus," I said sincerely and as normally as I could when I secretly wanted to jump up and down as giddy as I was at meeting "gods".

Achilles took my hand in his. "Take us to our chambers."

Erebus frowned at Achilles, but he shook his head and turned around. "This way, please."

Why were you so mean to him?

Don't let Erebus deceive you. He's extremely powerful and very conceited.

It seems as though vanity runs through most Sidhe's veins.

Achilles laughed and squeezed my hand. "You're right about that."

We walked through several stone hallways much like the ones in Zeus' castle before finally coming to a bedroom. Erebus stood on the outside of the bedroom and smiled. "Here it is."

I smiled back at him and walked inside. The room was decorated in various shades of blue and was as large as Darren's house had been. Achilles shut the door and then walked quickly to the dresser. He opened the drawers and pointed inside. "These are all yours."

I stepped forward and looked down into the drawers and at the various folded dresses and corsets. I pulled out a dress that matched my eyes and held it up in front of me in the mirror. "It's perfect."

Achilles whispered, "You're perfect."

I turned and looked up at him, furrowing my brow. He ran his thumb down my cheek and bent down, his lips a breadth away from mine when someone knocked on the bedroom door. He stepped back, and I walked quickly to the bathroom to put on the corset and dress. Luckily the corset was the kind you tightened and then simply zipped up. I smoothed the dress into place and adjusted the bodice a few times before I was happy with the placement. I smiled at my reflection in the mirror and touched a couple of the purple highlights. The dress definitely looked great with the highlights and my new skin designs. I stepped out of the bathroom and stared at the doorway where my older, blonder, more blue twin stood. At least we could have passed for twins in the human world, if she hadn't been blue, but with her in the same room as me I could feel the power she possessed and the difference in age. She stared to walk towards me, and I felt incredibly nervous.

"Hello, daughter," she said softly.

I swallowed and tried to fight the tears in my eyes. "Hello, mother."

Are you going to hug her?

I don't know. Should I hug her? Do you even think she wants to hug me?

Before I could decide, she rushed forward and hugged me against her, crying. "Oh, I've been such a fool."

We held on to each other for a few more minutes, each of us crying softly. When we pulled back she looked from me to Achilles and then back again. "Why are you able to communicate mind-to-mind?"

Achilles actually began looking nervous, he stepped back a few feet and said, "Well, you see Hera was upset and was trying to kill Artemis so I bound her..."

Athena was known by the humans as being the Goddess of Wisdom, the one who was the best strategic planner. As her skin began glowing, and she turned on Achilles, I could see why a Goddess of Wisdom would frighten you and you might consider worshipping her. "You bound her! How could you do such a thing?"

"Hera was going to kill me," I said in defense of Achilles.

Athena stopped glowing and looked at me. "Do you understand what it means to be bound?"

I shook my head and Achilles said, "I haven't had time to explain it to her."

Hera took the opportunity to walk into the bedroom. "Aw, I see you've been reunited with your daughter."

Athena nodded. "Yes, but Achilles was just about to explain to Artemis what it means to be…"

I held up my hand and looked at Achilles. "How long until Ares is here?"

Athena and Hera both gasped. Athena asked, "What do you know of Ares? Has he hurt you?"

Hera's skin began glowing. "He better not show his mongrel face in my court."

I looked at Achilles frantically. "You said he was going to meet us here. You said—"

Athena interrupted me to yell at Achilles. "You let Ares near her?"

Achilles held up his hand. "You'd better sit down." Athena and Hera sat in a pair of chairs I hadn't seen before. Achilles sat down on the edge of the bed and sighed. "Where to begin?"

Athena spoke through clenched teeth, "How about start at the part where Ares was near my daughter."

"Artemis met Ares before I had a chance to find her."

Hera looked at me. "Well, explain."

I folded my arms over my chest, feeling angry at their reaction of Ares and defensive of him. "I am not just Artemis of the Werewolves or Artemis, Darren's daughter. I am

Artemis Lupine, mate of Prince Ares of the Werewolves. I am Ares' *passt genau*."

Athena wailed and began crying. "No. No! It can't be true."

Hera stood and started towards me. Achilles stepped in her path and said, "You cannot kill her without killing me, too. We're bound, remember?"

I looked up at Achilles' back in shock. "What? What do you mean by that?"

Hera stomped back to her chair and tried to console Athena.

Achilles turned around and sighed. "I planned on telling you, but we haven't had time. When you're bound to someone if that person dies, then you die, too."

"So, if I die, you will die as well? Or if you die, then I die?"

He nodded.

"You're a fool! You should have let me die. I'm not worth your life!" I yelled. I wasn't ready to be responsible for someone else's life.

Athena sighed. "We should have killed her when we were supposed to. No, I should have never fallen for Darren."

I spun around and glared at her. "Ares is a good man. You have no reason to hate him like this. He has been great to me. Better than any of you have been!"

Athena stood up and glared back at me. "I will not allow my daughter to be mated with *him*."

My skin began glowing as I grew madder. "It's not your decision."

"The hell it isn't!"

"You lost the power to make decisions when you left me," I yelled at the top of my lungs.

She blinked at me a few times before stepping back and sighing. "I see the wolf is very present in you."

I gaped at her. "Just because I'm angry doesn't mean it's because of my wolf. You were just talking about how you should have killed me. What the hell is wrong with you people?"

Hera stood up and looked at me. "I will not allow you and Ares to bring another mixed blood into this world. Having two of you is bad enough. You will not be allowed to procreate."

My anger rose again and with it, my Sidhe powers. My wings popped out of my back, and my skin glowed brighter than usual. I started to levitate off of the ground and said, "I'd like to see you try and stop us."

Hera's body began glowing, and she began levitating as well. "One son is not worth a pair of mixed bloods breeding!"

I hadn't even felt him approaching, but then he was just there. A warm presence in the cold room. "Enough!" Ares yelled.

Hera spun around and glared at him. "You! Get the hell out of my Court!"

She started towards him, and I shot her in the back with a fireball. "Don't you dare touch my mate."

Achilles moved next to me and took my hand in his. "Artemis, please calm down. You do not need to fight."

Ares rushed forward and had Achilles in the air by his throat before I'd even blinked. "You had better do some quick explaining Achilles," Ares said through gritted teeth.

Achilles nodded, and Ares dropped him to the ground. Achilles rubbed his throat and whispered, "It was an emergency. Hera was the one attacking her in your meadow and she was sucking the life out of her. I only did it to save her."

Hera said, "I would have killed her if he hadn't done it. In fact, I'm still thinking about it."

Ares growled. "Unless you want a war with the were-wolves, I suggest you wipe that idea from your mind."

"Ares," I whispered.

Ares turned to me and for the first time really looked at me. He walked forward and grabbed a strand of my purple hair, looked at my wings behind me and then ran a fingertip along one of my new vines. "I wouldn't have thought it was possible, but you're even more beautiful now."

I released my Sidhe powers and put my wings away and hugged him. He hugged me tightly and kissed my lips. "I'm sorry, Ares," I said softly.

He stroked my hair and shushed me. "None of this is your fault, and we'll deal with the predicament Achilles has put us into later."

Athena hissed, "Step away from my daughter."

Ares and I turned to face her, and I said, "You don't get to pick and choose when I'm your daughter. Either you want me dead or you don't. You can't keep changing sides."

Hera sighed. "We should have killed Ares when we had that slut abort their baby."

Ares growled and his eyes turned golden. I turned to Hera. "You killed one of his children?"

Ares turned away from everyone as he tried to calm himself. Hera sat down in the chair again. "He seduced and mated with one of the Sidhe women. Halfbreeds are not allowed, you and Ares are...*exceptions*, but we have strict rules for a reason. We made her abort the abomination before it had a chance to develop into," she gestured at Ares, "this."

Koda, who I hadn't noticed until then, rushed forward and began trying to console Ares. Ares shrugged him off and turned around. The pain he felt leaked through our bond and it became too much for me. I could feel how much pain he was in, and it summoned my rage.

I ran forward and attacked Hera. She was quick though and dodged my first punch and managed to get up out of the chair and to a more open area. I attacked her with all of the training I'd received for my fight with Natasha. I opened three cuts on Hera before she managed to land a hit on me. She stumbled backwards, and before I could move to attack her again, Ares was in front of me and holding me. Achilles rushed forward and stood in front of Hera.

"Artemis. Sunshine. Look at me," Ares yelled.

I pushed against him, trying to get to Hera. I wanted more of her blood. More blood from the one hurting my mate.

"Artemis, this is no longer a battle. You can't save the baby, its dead. The mother has moved on and is happily mated to a new man. I've moved on and am happily mated to you. Please. Stop."

I stopped moving and looked up at him with tears in my eyes. "They killed your baby. They separated you from your mate."

He nodded. "Yes."

Tears leaked down my face. "They want to do it again."

"I know."

I growled, the sound rumbling my chest. "I won't let them."

Ares kissed my cheek. "I know."

His tenderness stole my rage, and I sagged against him, letting him hold me up against his body. He kissed my forehead and rubbed my back slowly as tears leaked down my face from the emotions we were sharing.

Ares and I regained our composure and turned back to Hera and Athena. I whispered, "You do not get to decide who we mate with. You do not get to decide if we breed or not. If you try to separate us, we'll consider it an act of war against the werewolves. If we have children and you try to hurt them, we will consider it an assassination attempt and thus an act of war. Do I make myself clear?"

Hera glared at me a moment before saying, "You've learned a lot in a short time. I understand your views. I've heard your statements."

Athena stood up and smoothed her dress down. "We'll leave you alone now." She turned and left with Hera without a second glance back at me.

Ares rubbed my back and asked, "Want to stir up some gossip?"

I looked up at his smiling face. The change of subject so quick it made my head spin. "What?"

He tugged on my hand. "Come on. It's been a century since I've been here. Let's go walk around so you can see everything and people can have something new to gossip about."

I shook my head. "You always surprise me."

Ares laughed. "Oh, this is only the beginning, Sunshine."

Ares took my hand and lead me back through the castle hallways and then out a pair of large wooden doors. I'd expected a similar scene as the Dark Court, but the Light Court was different. Waterfalls, at least a hundred feet tall made a wall to the left. The waterfalls fell into a beautiful river that flowed through the center of the realm. Vines with beautiful flowers covered every building. The buildings seemed to be carved trees or trees grown into the shape of buildings.

Ares whispered, "A few of the Sidhe are gifted with nature abilities. They were able to charm the growing trees into the shapes of their buildings. The buildings, now being centuries old, are as sturdy as any rock fortress."

I sat down on a wooden bench and looked at Ares. "Who is your father?"

Ares turned and looked at me in shock. "What?"

I turned away from him and looked at the waterfall, suddenly nervous. "I know what you are."

"Oh." Ares sat down beside me and sighed loudly. "Who told you?"

"I figured it out by your name."

"I had planned on telling you later."

"Who is your father?" I asked again.

"Zeus."

I blinked at him and then laughed. "Of course! That's why you and Achilles look so much alike! Wow, I can't believe I didn't put two and two together sooner."

Ares picked my hand up gently and rubbed his thumb across my knuckles. "Are you mad at me?"

I closed my eyes as I enjoyed his simple touch. "Yes."

He bent and kissed my neck, nibbling lightly. "How about now?"

I growled softly. "Yes."

Ares laughed and stood up and started walking again. I caught up to him and linked hands. "Do you have any abilities?" I asked him as we continued through the town.

Ares sighed and looked up at the waterfall. "It was scandalous enough that Zeus bred with a werewolf female, but when his son showed no signs of power besides that of his wolf side, the Sidhe couldn't take it. I spent fifty years in the Dark and Light Courts only to be cast out after finding a mate who loved me even though I had no powers. I can't blame her for following the Queen's order. She would be terribly lonely in the human world and she would be especially sad to know that you were my true mate."

"How can I be your true mate if you already had a mate?"

"We broke our mate bond a long time ago. Many years before your parents even met, so technically I had no mate."

"Was she beautiful?" I asked as I looked around at the gorgeous Sidhe women walking around.

Ares stopped me and turned me to face him. "There are many beautiful women in the world, Artemis, but none as beautiful and as wonderful as you."

"I have something I want to do, but I think you're not going to like it." I'd been thinking about it privately the past couple of days.

"What is that?" he asked as he pushed my hair behind my ear.

"Maurice wants to wipe out the humans. He wants them extinct. I can't let that happen. There has to be some way for us to save them, or as many of them as we can."

"He's not killing all of them. The humans are given a choice, be turned into a vampire or werewolf, be slaves, or be killed. The humans decide."

I frowned at him. "You do realize that most humans will simply choose death?"

Ares shrugged. "It's their choice."

"I can help them. If they see me and see that there are other races who aren't bloodthirsty vampires, more will choose to live."

Ares stared at me for a few moments before sighing. "Why do I get the feeling that you'll do this with or without me?"

I kissed his lips softly and whispered, "Because we're getting to know each other better. I have to try to save as many as I can. Humans should be allowed to be free, not just slaves."

Ares shrugged. "Alright. We'll go to the places left in Europe and try to save as many as we can."

I hugged him tightly and kissed his cheek. "I love you."

He laughed and hugged me back. "I love you, too. Now come on let's get back before Achilles has a brain hemorrhage from being separated from you."

I stopped him before he could take a step and whispered, "There's something I need to tell you."

Ares nodded. "Go on."

I let go of his hand and turned away from him, looking at the magnificent waterfalls. "I released Achilles' powers with just a touch. He said it means I'm his destined mate."

Ares was eerily silent. I turned around and found him glaring down at the ground. His hands were clenched into fists and I could hear his teeth grinding against each other. "When did this happen?"

"At your meadow, before you found us. I know you told me not to touch him, but I was just so mesmerized by his vines that I ran my fingertip along one and…"

"Have you kissed him? Or mated with him?" he asked as he continued to stare at the ground.

I rushed forward and picked Ares' fists up in my hands and looked up into his face where I saw not anger, but fear. "No. Of course not, Ares. You're my mate and I'd never cheat on you."

Ares teeth clenched again and he said, "He's also your mate. You're going to have the same impulses for him as you did for me. Will you fight it like you did me?"

I collapsed against Ares and sobbed once. "I don't know. I don't know what to do." I looked up at him and saw compassion now in his eyes. "What do you want me to do?"

Ares smiled and then shook his head laughing. "No, I'm

not going to be evil. If you need to touch him, then go ahead, but until Achilles and I talk, I'd appreciate it if you didn't do anything with him beyond that."

I wrapped my arms around him and hugged him tight. "Okay. Ares, for what it's worth, I am sorry."

Ares wrapped his arms around me in a tight hug. "It's worth a lot to me. Thank you."

We walked back in silence, enjoying the peace for once and being able to be in each other's presence. We walked into Achilles' room to find Hera, Achilles, and Koda inside arguing vehemently.

"What's this about?" Ares asked.

Achilles glared at Ares. "You agreed to help her? How could you agree to a suicide mission? The humans are as likely to kill her as they are to listen to her!"

"I'll be beside her to protect her. No human will harm her with me there," Ares said through gritted teeth.

Achilles threw his hands up into the air.

"Achilles, you have to understand why I want to…"

The wall beside Ares and I exploded. Ares spun around and dropped to the ground, his body covering mine from the debris. Ares jumped back up and I gaped at the wolves growling at us. Ares growled. "Stupid vampires."

Hera yelled, "Guards!" but there was no need because a battle was already under way in the hallways. Ares ran forward and grabbed one of the wolves by its neck, quickly snapping the spine and killing it. The body reverted to the vampires' true form, with their scary face and six inch dagger fingers.

Ares turned to Hera. "These are not werewolves. They're vampires taking wolf form."

Hera nodded. "I witnessed your truth."

Ares smiled. "I'll assist in your defense."

Hera sighed dramatically. "Very well."

Ares kissed my cheek and pushed me into Koda's arms. "Take care of her."

Achilles and Ares ran side by side out the hole in the wall and began fighting with vampires and vampires in wolf form.

EIGHT

Watching Achilles and Ares fight side by side was an incredible turn on. I fought to control my hormones, but it was difficult, especially since both were my destined mate.

Koda tossed me on to the bed and shook his body. "I really wish you wouldn't think about things like that when I'm touching you. I'd rather not get in trouble with Ares. Again."

I blushed and adjusted myself on the bed. "I'm sorry."

The fight was over relatively quickly, with the vampires stopping the wolf charade and fleeing. Ares came back into the room, and I ran forward to hug him. He kissed my cheek and set me back down on the ground. "You shouldn't worry so much, Artemis."

I sighed. "I know, but I can't help it."

Achilles stopped near me, and I reached out to lay my hand on his arm. Ares' jaw clenched, but he stayed still. Achilles smiled at me in thanks then moved across the room to give Ares and I space.

Hera asked, "Why would the vampires attack here?"

"To start a war between the Sidhe and werewolves of course." Ares frowned.

Achilles folded his arms across his chest. "Surely they knew that there are connections within our races. They have to know that I would contact you to discuss this."

Ares rolled his eyes. "Because we are *so* fond of each other."

Achilles smiled. "Well, neither of us would have lied about something as serious as this. I could always tell when you were lying."

"Ares!" yelled a familiar voice.

Ares pushed me to the side of him and we both stared in shock at a group of Sidhe guards holding Matt between them.

Ares started to growl and then caught himself. "Release my brother."

Erebus, one of the guards holding Matt, shook his head. "I'm sorry, Ares, but we can't do that. We found him holding the portal open. He's the one who let the vampires in and out."

Ares blinked a few times and then looked at Matt. "Is this true?"

Matt growled. "All they wanted was her! All you had to do was just give her to them!"

Ares took a step forward and asked, "Why would you betray me? What have I done worthy of your treachery?"

"Did you really think I would stand by and watch you in mated bliss while I was forced to be your guard?" Matt asked. "She's nothing more than a mistake. She should have been put down. *You* should have put her down when you found her. You know what she will be capable of! Her being your match has blinded you. Love has blinded you!"

Ares took another step forward, his fury building. "Each

time those vampires and dhampirs found us. You told them where we were, didn't you?"

Matt bowed his head in defeat. "Yes." I could see he was holding something back. Even during his hate filled tirade he hadn't seemed sincerely angry. What could he be holding back from us? Why would he want me killed?

Tears sprang to my eyes and I walked closer to Matt. "Why would you do this? I've never been anything other than loving to you. I trusted you with my life. I loved you as a brother."

Matt looked at me, and I could see the regret in his eyes. "I had to. They have something of mine that I cannot live without. Surely you would do the same if Ares' life were in danger."

He *had* been holding out. I shook my head. "I would not substitute the life of a friend for the life of Ares and Ares would not want me to. Would you have done the same if it were Koda you had to hand over?"

Matt's eyes flared gold and he snarled. "No."

"Then why me, Matt? Why were you willing to let me die for whoever they have?" I asked as sorrow filled my body. I had never felt so hurt, so betrayed by someone before.

"There was no other way. I had to give you to them. He promised he wouldn't hurt you. He just needed you in his possession." Tears spilled down his cheeks as he looked at me. "You must know that there is no way to defeat him. He will get you one way or another. The only hope is to join him."

Ares took a step towards him and asked, "Who are you working for?"

Matt tried to pull out of the guards holds, but they held him in place. "The one who will rule the world whether he uses Artemis or kills her," Matt answered when he realized he wasn't getting away.

Why was he switching between moods so quickly? "Ares, I think he's tied to someone."

Koda walked up to Matt and inhaled his brother's head. He snarled and then turned, sadness and anger twisting his face. "He's been bitten."

Ares rushed forward and grabbed Matt by the throat, choking him. "Who do you work for? Tell me his name!"

Matt whispered, "Maurice."

Ares released Matt and walked towards me. "You were right. He wants to rule the world and knows of the prophecy."

"What prophecy?" I asked.

Ares shook his head and started back towards Matt. "Another time. First, I have to deal with this…"

The guards shoved Matt down on to his knees and held him as he struggled against them. Ares started to reach out towards him, but Achilles walked forward and held out his sword to Ares. "Here, this is more efficient and not nearly as messy as ripping off his head."

Matt began to whine. "Please Ares. Don't kill me. I love you. I wouldn't have done this if there had been another way. Surely you see that there was no other way!"

Ares snarled. "There is *always* another way. You could have come to me. We could have figured this out together. Instead you betrayed us all."

"No, Ares. Please." Matt begged.

I knew what Matt had done was awful, but part of me wanted to forgive him. There had to be some other punishment.

I started to move forward, but Koda grabbed me and held me back. "Matt, I loved you. I would have died for you," I whispered as tears fell down my cheeks.

Matt met my eyes and whispered, "Now is your first

lesson. Trust few and guard your heart. I'm sorry Artemis. I truly am."

Ares took Achilles' offered sword and stood next to Matt. "I loved you as my pack mate. I loved you as my brother. You betrayed your alpha. You betrayed your pack sister. You betrayed all werewolves by assisting the vampire who wants to rule the world. Your punishment is death." Ares raised the sword over Matt's neck, pain and anger twisting his handsome features.

Koda hugged me tightly against him. Our bodies shook against each other as we prepared for our friend, our loved one to die.

Ares whispered, "I am sorry, Matthew. I should have seen the signs. I failed as your alpha and as your brother. I am sorry it had to end like this. May you run forever in the forests of the afterlife."

Ares started to lower the sword, and I turned my head into Koda's chest, clenching my eyes closed and knowing that would not block the pain I felt.

The instant Matt's life ended, I felt it like a blow to the chest. Koda and I collapsed to the floor, still clinging to each other. I wailed my sorrow and Koda shifted to his wolf form and howled his.

I buried my face in his fur as I cried and felt the dagger of loss and also the heat of anger at his betrayal of us. It hurt so much and I could do nothing to ease the pain.

Ares dropped to his knees beside us. I looked up and saw unshed tears in his eyes and knew he was hurt from Matt's death as well, but it was a necessary evil he had to have endured many times. Matt being his brother though must have hurt the most.

I wrapped one arm around him and the other I draped

over Koda's back. Koda howled again and Ares' human throat enlarged to form a wolf's in order to howl. My throat changed suddenly and then I was howling, too. My pack howled our sorrow at the loss of their brother, our hearts bleeding from his death.

I WOKE THE NEXT MORNING, my throat, eyes, and head sore from the howling, sobbing, and sniveling. I'd never experienced someone's death as I had with Matt's. There was a small space within me that felt as if it would never heal. I couldn't even begin to imagine how Ares and Koda were feeling, especially since both were acting as though nothing had happened. Achilles and Ares were talking quietly together while Koda sat next to me in the bed, reading a magazine. I sat up and stretched and Koda whispered, "Morning. Would you like some water?"

I nodded, and he handed me a glass of water from the side table. Ares stopped talking with Achilles to come over and give me a quick kiss on the lips. "If you want, go take a shower and freshen up. We're discussing our next move."

After grabbing another dress and corset from the dresser, I walked to the bathroom and stared at my haggard reflection. Dark bags hung under my eyes, which were bloodshot and nasty looking. I quickly stripped out of my clothes and started the shower.

The warm water felt amazing against my skin and helped clear my head. I wasn't sure what Achilles and Ares were discussing, but there was only one clear course of action in my mind. We had to get in touch with Victor and then face Maurice together. I knew it would involve a battle, and we would probably die, but it was the only way to stop all of this. I couldn't live the rest of my life with him sending hordes of minions after me. He wanted me, dead or alive, but I only wanted him dead. So, either he was dead, or I was.

I finished my shower and bathroom necessities and after dressing, walked out to the sitting area where Achilles and Ares were. "Can you get a hold of Victor?"

Ares frowned at me. "We already have, he is going to meet us here in five days."

I smiled. "Good."

Achilles frowned at me, Ares' and his looks remarkably similar, making me a fool for not noticing the relation sooner. "What are you planning?" Ares asked me.

I sat down beside Ares and sipped on the water Koda had given me. "Nothing. So, between now and when Victor comes, are we going to work on my plan?"

Ares and Achilles looked at me and then at each other.

With only four days to save as many humans as possible, I felt rushed. How was I going to keep the humans safe? How many could I truly save?

It was far away from our current location, but I knew the first place I had to go. "I want to leave in twenty minutes. Please don't argue with me. Please just get ready and come with me," I said to the three men in the room. Ares and Achilles watched me with worried expressions, but said nothing. Finally, both men stood up and began preparing to leave.

I sat on the bed and felt my nerves growing. There were so many things happening that it felt as though my nerves had been flayed open. My hands shook softly as I thought about talking to a group of humans and trying to convince them to listen to me.

"It'll be alright, Darlin'," Koda said as he rubbed his hands up and down my arms. "I think what you're doing is great."

"Is anyone else trying to save humans?" I asked as I leaned back against him, letting his touch and smell calm me.

Koda continued to rub my arms as he talked. "Everyone is allowed humans as slaves. The humans report to the camps and say, 'I'm Koda's slave' and they're kept alive and fed until we claim them. Those of us with a lot more power and thus a lot more slaves decide on a brand and for those humans we want as slaves, we brand them. So, we say the humans are our slaves, but when everything is said and done we let them go free. There aren't many of us who will let them go free."

That was how I would keep them free. I'd convince the humans to use Ares' brand and say they were his slaves. It wasn't the best plan, but it was a start.

"We're ready," Ares said from beside me.

I turned and found him dressed in sweatpants and a t-shirt. It was strange to see sweatpants strained to the point of breaking around his leg muscles. Every boy at my high school had been practically swimming in their sweatpants.

"What?" Ares asked as he looked at his clothes.

I shook my head. "Nothing, just comparing you to boys at my school and finding I'm extremely lucky."

Ares held his hand out, and I took it, standing up from the bed and walking into the circle of his arms. "I love you, Artemis."

"I love you too, Ares." His body was radiating more heat than normal and it felt good to be held by him. I pulled out of his arms reluctantly and turned to smile at Achilles. "I guess it's harder for Sidhe men to wear shirts."

Achilles smiled. "I could wear a shirt, but I prefer not to destroy clothes when releasing my wings."

Slowly, I walked to him and wrapped my arms around him. His body was stiff at first, but after a moment he relaxed and hugged me back. "I'm not used to this connection yet, but I've learned from being with Ares that it's better to give in and touch you then deal with the itching skin and irritation."

Achilles kissed the top of my head and whispered, "Thank you."

I pulled out of his arms and turned to face all three men. "I know you probably don't agree with what I'm doing, or at least are worried about my safety, but I have to do this or I'll regret it for the rest of my life."

Ares smiled. "We understand, Artemis."

Achilles cleared his throat and said, "Hephaestus, I require your assistance."

Two seconds later someone knocked on the door and then a man with forearms the size of my waist walked into the room. "You summoned me, Prince?"

Achilles stepped forward. "Artemis and Ares need a brand for selecting their human slaves. I'd appreciate your assistance in this matter."

Hephaestus looked at Ares and smiled. "Hello, Ares."

Ares smiled. "Hello, Hephaestus. You're looking well."

Hephaestus walked closer to me and then dropped to one knee and bowed. "It's an honor to meet you, Princess Artemis."

"Please, just call me Artemis."

He stood up and looked from me to Ares. "You want something simple or something dramatic?" he asked Ares.

Ares smiled. "Simple, if possible, yet still able to be easily recognizable from any others."

Hephaestus nodded. "Be back in fifteen minutes."

He walked out of our room through the giant hole in our wall and disappeared down the hallway.

Ares tugged me towards the table and pointed at the fruits and cheeses. "You need to eat anyways, so you might as well do it while he is making our brand."

I gave in and sat down, piling my plate high with food and then consuming the entire thing before Hephaestus came back.

Hephaestus held a cloth-wrapped bundle in his hands and smiled at us. "You didn't give me much time to work on it, but I hope you like it." He placed the bundle on the table before me and slowly unrolled the cloth. I pushed aside my empty plate and watched eagerly for the reveal.

I don't know what I was expecting, but the short, one-foot brand with a crescent moon and starburst was not it. It was beautiful. I said as much, which earned me a big smile from Hephaestus.

I stroked the moon and starburst brand and Ares said, "The moon and star are very fitting for us. I couldn't have picked a better design. We need you to make twenty replicas as soon as possible please."

Hephaestus laughed. "I should have known. Give me ten minutes to make them."

After Hephaestus left again, I turned to Achilles. "Can he really make twenty of these in ten minutes?"

Achilles nodded. "His greatest feat was making Ares five hundred swords in one hour."

That made my mouth drop. Five hundred swords in one hour? How is that humanly.... well there is the answer. Humans could never do such a thing, which is why they used to worship the Sidhe.

Ares sat down in a large chair and waved me over. I came over and sat down on his lap, sighing happily as he wrapped his arms around me. These little moments of relaxation with him were my favorite. Ares put his lips against my ear and began whispering too low for anyone else to hear. "You look so beautiful and smell so good. No woman on this earth can compare to you." Ares kissed my cheek and then nuzzled behind my ear, making me shiver. "I love you and hate the moments when we're separated. If it were up to me, I'd take you to the most remote place on earth so that we could be completely alone all the time."

I giggled and shook my head. "As long as it's not anywhere too hot or too cold."

Ares laughed. "But if it's cold it gives me an excuse to cuddle with you more."

I turned and nuzzled his ear with my nose, inhaling his scent. "I do like the sound of that."

Hephaestus came back with a wooden box in his arms and smiled at us. "Here you go. Twenty brands."

Ares stood, putting me back on the seat before taking the box and bowing to him. "Thank you."

Hephaestus bowed and smiled at Ares. "Anything for an old friend. Of course, you'll let me know if any battles are coming up with need of my skills?"

Ares laughed. "You'll be the first one I contact."

Hephaestus said goodbye and left.

Ares picked up the brands and asked, "So, where to first?"

"Where I was raised," I answered quickly.

Ares picked my hand up and kissed the back of it. "Alright, let's go."

We started to walk towards the door when it was flung

open and Hera stepped through. "Good, I caught you before you left."

Ares and I looked at each other and then at her. "How'd you know we were leaving?" I asked suspiciously.

Hera waved her hand dismissively. "I'm Queen for a reason, dear. Now, I may not agree fully with what you're doing, but I'll agree to help."

Achilles walked forward and asked, "Help how?"

She smiled sweetly at him. "You shouldn't be so suspicious of your own mother. Of course, I did train you to be weary of everyone so I suppose that's my fault." She stood still a moment, thinking and then waved her hand dismissively. "Anyways, I'll travel with you so that we can teleport and get to every place faster."

She had to have another motive, but being able to teleport would make things much easier. "Alright," I said.

She clapped her hands together. "Wonderful. Alright, everyone join hands."

After forming a circle, Hera put her hands on Achilles and me who were on either side of her and she whispered, "Don't throw up on me." The world turned black and then we started spinning out of control. I gripped Ares' hand hard as I fought the nausea. The world came back into focus, and we stood outside the bar in the town I'd been raised in.

I pulled my hands free of everyone and looked around at the town. All of the houses were dark and the only light came from the bar. Where was everyone? It was night time, but it wasn't late enough that everyone should be in bed.

I heard shouting and arguments from inside the bar and turned to Ares and the rest of our group. "Ares, you come with me, but everyone else, please go wait in the trees. I'll bring them out here."

Ares handed the box of brands to Koda, picked up my hand and together we walked to the bar door. I stopped in front of it and took a deep breath. It was now or never. I pushed open the door and found the entire town inside, crammed together as they argued. All eyes turned to me and everyone stopped talking.

Billy's mouth dropped open as he looked at the vines on my skin and the purple in my hair and my purple eyes.

I straightened my back and looked at each pair of eyes. "You all know about the killings going on around the world. I've come to save as many of you as I can."

Skankzilla, my old arch nemesis, put her hands on her hips and glared at me. "And how are *you* going to save us?"

I smiled at her and said, "Everyone outside. I'll prove to you that I'm capable of much more than you think I am." I turned and Ares and I walked out of the bar, letting them all follow us. I knew they would follow because, well, what else would they do? I stopped when I reached a big enough open area that they could all gather and see me without being too close. I trusted most of them, but that didn't mean that they wouldn't freak out and try to hurt me.

Ares released my hand and took a couple steps away from me to give him more room to maneuver if he needed to stop any of them from coming after me. I could feel Koda and Achilles behind us in the trees, waiting. Everyone finally gathered near me in the clearing, murmuring nervously to each other. I took a deep breath and said, "You're going to be given a couple options by those coming, but I'm here to give you another option. Freedom."

People looked at each other in shock and then Billy asked, "What do you mean?"

I looked at Ares and he nodded. I turned back to the group

and said, "We've been kept in the dark for centuries about the existence of preternaturals. Now, the preternaturals are taking the world back, taking control. Millions of humans have already been killed as you've seen from the news reports. The mist is vampires and the wolves are werewolves."

The group began murmuring loudly and then Glen, the oldest man in our town, stepped forward. "How do we know you're telling the truth? And if you are, what do you want from us?"

"I'll prove to you that preternaturals exist and all I want is for you to trust me and do what I say." I turned to the trees and said, "Come out. I don't really think we need all of us, but it'll be better to show them that it's not just me who's different."

Koda, Achilles and Hera came forward, standing just behind me. I closed my eyes and focused on the flame within me that was my source of power. I opened my eyes and knew my body was glowing.

I dimmed the light so that they could see me as I pulled my wings from my back. The crowd gasped in shock and everyone took a step back. "Don't be afraid. I won't harm you."

"What are you?" Skankzilla asked.

"I'm half werewolf and half Sidhe, or fairy as you call us."

"Werewolf?" Billy asked. "You don't look like a wolf."

His tone was mocking, as if he expected me to be lying about it. He could see me glowing with wings out of my back, but he still doubted I could be a werewolf. Had I been that dense?

Yes. Yes I had.

Ares said, "Artemis is telling the truth. She and I are the only mixed bloods. The only half werewolf, half Sidhe." He pulled his shirt off and I glared at Skankzilla who all but trampled those in front of her to get a better look. Ares kept his sweatpants on and took a half-shift. Koda came to stand beside Ares and changed into his wolf form.

A woman in the back screamed and I released my powers, letting my wings retract and said, "Don't be frightened. Ares and Koda won't harm anyone. They're simply showing you the forms we can take. As you can see, werewolves do exist."

Ares reverted back to his human form and shook his body like a dog flinging water off.

"In a short amount of time, a group of preternaturals, the vampires and wolves, will come to this town. They will give you the options of death, becoming one of them or becoming slaves," I continued.

I took one of the brands from the box Koda was holding and set it on the ground in front of me. "If you don't want to be turned, if you want to stay free, use this brand and they'll know you are Prince Ares of the Werewolves' slaves."

"How does us being your slave make us free?" Glen asked.

"Because I won't keep you as slaves. When things have cooled off we will let you go and you'll all be free," Ares said as he took my hand.

I looked at Billy and said, "Please. You have to listen to me. I lived with you all thinking I was human like you. What I've seen since then has changed me, but I'm still your friend. Please, do what I'm asking."

Hera put her hands on us and Koda and Achilles put their hands on her. "Heed Artemis' advice, humans."

I'd wanted to say more, but Hera had probably been right to make us leave. Though I would have liked to talk to some of the people in town whom I knew would listen to reason.

The nausea vanished and I opened my eyes to find us in a

large plaza filled with people. I stood up on top of a table and yelled to get everyone's attention. "Listen to me! Everyone!"

∾

WE TRAVELED from place to place, only sparing an hour or so to nap once in a while. Once we went to the last places left in America, we returned to Europe.

I stood in the Coliseum and raised my hands and wings up. "They're coming and there is only one way to stay free." Achilles translated for me as I spoke. "Choose to be our slaves and we will grant you freedom once everything is settled. If you agree, just use this brand on your arm and you will be spared."

Each time I finished my speech Hera teleported us out. It was great for time, but it also made our point to the humans that we really were telling the truth. We weren't human and we had powers they thought were reserved for fairytales and movies.

I looked up at our new location and blinked in shock. Russia. Since fully gaining my Sidhe powers, the cold didn't bother me as much anymore so I ignored the cold and looked at the beautiful snow. I walked around and looked at the buildings in awe. It was night time and there weren't many humans out so I couldn't make my speech now. "Maybe we should wait until tomorrow?" I suggested.

Ares rubbed his thumb across my knuckles. "Tomorrow is our last day."

I leaned against him, exhausted from the traveling and lack of sleep. "I know."

Ares led us through the streets and to an older building. After talking with the security guard for a moment, he let us in. Ares took us the top floor where a large penthouse took up the entire floor. I looked at Ares and he smiled. "I have a few buildings around the world. This is one of mine."

"You own this?"

He nodded.

I walked around and looked at the elaborate decorations and the set up. It was gorgeous and everything looked expensive. Even the light fixtures seemed to be made out of gold and jewels. I walked to the master bedroom and stared at the bed that seemed to be three king sized mattresses put together. The bed took up the entire room and I jumped up on to it as soon as I entered. The comforter was filled with down feathers and the mattress was like lying on clouds.

Ares hopped up on the bed beside me and kissed my cheek. "We should get some food before we go to sleep."

I nodded and sighed happily. "I think this is the most comfortable bed I've ever laid on."

Koda laughed. "It better be! Ares spent a lot to have this bed made."

Hera cleared her throat to get our attention. "There's a café just down the street that stays open late."

Ares helped me climb out of the bed and we all walked back out of the building and to the café. We all sat in a booth and I looked around at the faces of those with me and couldn't help laughing.

"What's so funny?" Koda asked.

"Here we are in the human world, sitting in a café with the Queen of the Light Court of the Sidhe, the Prince of the Werewolves, the Prince of the Sidhe and, well, me and you. It's just funny to me that after so many years of being human now I'm sitting here with all of you and it feels like its no big deal."

Ares slipped his arm around my waist. "You're adjusting,

which is good. If you weren't adjusting that would be bad. Though, I do see your point and it is somewhat funny."

My mood sobered and I asked, "Do you think anyone will listen to me?"

Achilles whispered, "It's their decision now, Artemis. Even if they don't believe you now, when the others come to capture them, they'll know you were telling the truth. You're doing the right thing in giving them a choice. Not many of the preternaturals would give the humans a choice."

We ate in silence and then returned to Ares' building to sleep. I only had one more day to travel, which meant only a few more places we could visit. Even though I knew Achilles was right, I felt as though I wasn't doing enough. As if there was something more that I could do. Something I could do to save *all* of humankind.

ARES WOKE me up by gently rubbing my back. "Mmm," I said half-consciously. He started to pull the blankets down, but I held on tight. "Cold," I protested.

Ares nipped my earlobe, successfully waking me up. "Come on. I have a surprise for you."

I wanted to groan and protest, but I was too curious to do either. After stretching and forcing myself up and out of the bed, I pulled on clothes and shuffled to the bathroom like a zombie, arms raised in front of me to avoid running into anything and feet shuffling across the carpet. I think I even moaned a little, which earned soft laughter from Ares' direction. I ignored him and hurriedly brushed my teeth and used the restroom before returning to him.

Ares hugged me against him and kissed my cheek. "I didn't know that you were also part zombie."

I snarled at him. "I am NOT a morning person." I looked towards the window and my mouth agape. "The sun isn't even out yet! It is way too early to be up."

Ares' fingers intertwined with mine, and he kissed my lips gently. "Come on. You'll forget all about the time when you see what I have planned."

I doubted him, but obligingly followed. Besides, any time I got to spend alone with Ares was worth the loss of sleep. We walked silently out of the bedroom, past Koda, Achilles and Hera, who were all sleeping peacefully, and out into the hall-way. Ares pushed open a door that had a sign with some type of warning, but I couldn't read Russian to decipher it's meaning.

"Ares, where are we going?"

He smiled his full, true smile I cherished so much and said, "It's a surprise."

I hated surprises, but for him and for that smile, I'd endure. We walked up a set of stairs and then Ares pushed open a door and we stepped out onto the roof of the building. The view was spectacular, even at night. I walked around the roof, but avoided getting too close to the edge. Even though I had wings now, I couldn't stand the thought of leaning out over the edge of the building.

Ares cleared his throat and I turned to find a blanket set on the snow covered roof with a picnic basket and wine. Ares had also set up two candles beside the blanket. I walked over to him and snapped my fingers, a small flame flickering to life above my finger, and lit the candles. I sat on the blanket beside Ares as he pulled out bread and cheese from the basket. He ripped a piece of the bread off and handed it to me. "It's come to my attention that we rarely have any alone time together. I intend to change that."

I took a bite of the warm bread and listened to him. He was right. We hardly ever got to enjoy time alone together. If he could arrange more dates like this, I was going to be a very happy woman.

"I'm sorry the beginning of your life with the preternaturals has been so difficult. I hope you know that I will do everything within my power to make up for this once the world has settled down."

I swallowed the bread and moved closer to him on the blanket, looking up into his blue eyes. "And how do you intend to make up for this?"

He smiled and my heart skipped a beat. "That is a need to know basis and you don't need to know. Yet."

I laughed and kissed his lips softly. "Tease."

The sun began to rise, and my breath caught in my throat as the lights changed colors in the sky and the buildings around us lit up. It was gorgeous.

Ares wrapped his arms around me and whispered, "I love you and every time I see the sun, I'll think of you, my Sunshine."

I relaxed against him and watched the sun rise, it was the best morning I'd had in a while. Ares and I ate the bread and cheese and then watched as the city's inhabitants began to rise.

"Ares?"

"Hm?"

"I have so many unanswered questions and it seems like I never have time to ask them. I don't want to ruin our date, but…"

Ares nodded. "You're right. Ask away."

I tried to think what to ask him first and my brain decided to draw blanks. I sat in the early morning light thinking for two full minutes until the first question popped into my head. "What's the prophecy you've talked about?"

Ares shifted until he was leaning back on his elbows and squinting at the sun. "Two hundred years ago an oracle made a prophecy which rocked the entire preternatural world. The oracle said, 'a mixed blood woman of great power will fight the evil which holds the world in darkness and right the balance of good and evil'. Many were confused since the current times weren't in darkness and so, we took it as an omen for the future. Most people forgot about the prophecy and decided the oracle was losing her touch and simply looking for attention. Now, it seems you may be the woman she was talking about."

"But the world isn't really unbalanced right now. I mean, I know the humans aren't ruling anymore, but that doesn't mean that the balance of good and evil is, well, unbalanced."

"Perhaps not right now, but if Maurice succeeds, he may tilt the balance."

Of course. "So, he wants me because he believes that after his plan is underway, I will be the only one capable of ending his tyranny?"

Ares wrapped his arms around me, growling softly. "I won't let him have you."

It was a very possessive gesture, but I scooted closer to him and allowed myself to relax in his hold. Strangely I enjoyed the possessiveness he showed. "I know. I trust you."

Ares rubbed his face against my hair and growled again. "Mine."

I leaned against him with all my weight, surprising him and forcing him onto his back. I straddled his body and pinned his arms down with my hands. "Mine." I nuzzled his neck and flicked my tongue along his pulse.

He smiled happily and pulled me down to squish me against his chest in a tight hug. "Yes. Forever."

I struggled out of his hold and then nipped his ear playfully before jumping away from him and squatting down. Ares sat up and smiled. I had to stop myself from shaking my butt since I didn't have a tail to wag and instead put my hands down in the snow of the rooftop and whined. Ares dashed towards me, and I tossed the snow I had in his face. He sputtered and wiped the snow off, but I was on the other side of the roof already, gathering up a snowball. He turned to me and I threw the ball, hitting him in the center of the chest. He looked down at the watery ball and watched as it slid down his stomach and to the ground.

He squatted down and began packing snow into a ball. "You asked for it now. You do realize this means war?"

I giggled and packed my own ball. "Bring it on, Your Highness."

His ball hit me in the stomach just as I threw mine and hit his shoulder. We both grabbed more ammunition and continued firing at each other. I packed my ball and aimed carefully, throwing it and watching with pure delight as it hit him on the head. The ball slid down his hair and plopped onto his shoulder.

I couldn't help it, I doubled over with laughter.

"You think that's funny?" Ares asked. I looked up at him, but couldn't stop laughing so I just nodded. His body blurred and I watched as he covered the distance of the roof to me in under one second. His body pressed up against mine as he smashed snow on the top of my head and squished it into my hair.

I gasped and pushed away from him, shaking my hair and trying to get the cold snow out. He laughed and returned to his side of the roof. I noticed he was inching towards the door and quickly threw the ball at him. At that moment, the door flung open, Achilles stepped out, and the snow ball hit him right in the face.

My hands covered my mouth as I fought not to laugh. The fight didn't last long as both Ares and I broke down and laughed hysterically. Achilles wiped the snow from his face and looked from me to Ares. "Now I understand what all the raucous was." He bent down and started making a large snow ball.

I shook my head and held up my hand. "No, Achilles, don't you even…" He tossed the large ball with deadly accuracy. It hit me in the chest and knocked me off my feet. I groaned as I sat up and glared at the laughing princes who seemed for the first time to have forgotten their differences as they shared a laugh at my expense. I made two balls and threw them at the two men, making them stop laughing and wipe at their faces.

Achilles looked at Ares. "Alliance?"

Ares smiled at Achilles. "Alliance."

Well, that couldn't be good. "Hey, no teaming up its not…" I screeched as I was forced to duck from the first few balls they tossed at me. I glared at the two men, but when I saw their smiling faces and saw them working together for the first time in who knew how many years, I couldn't get mad. So, I dodged as many of their balls as I could while throwing my own at them. We were all laughing and smiling until Hera walked out onto the roof with Koda and ruined our escapade by glaring at us. "It's time to eat and then you will speak to the last group of humans before we return."

"What a buzzkill she turned out to be," I muttered under

my breath. Unfortunately, I'd forgotten that she had enhanced hearing just like everyone else with me. Koda snickered then tried to play it off as a cough, while Achilles and Ares worked to keep straight faces.

Hera rolled her eyes and huffed, *"Children."*

CHAPTER

NINE

I was exhausted from all of our traveling. None of the humans had tried to attack me, though some had been frightened. I couldn't know how many I'd saved, if any, until after it was all done, but I felt good for trying. We returned to the Light Court and Achilles' chambers.

I lay in the bed between Achilles and Ares who had agreed to share the bed with me so that both could touch me while they slept. I stared up at the ceiling and wondered how we were going to work out something between the three of us. I knew I couldn't be with both Ares and Achilles, but my heart and the magic binding us didn't. Achilles suggested a fifty-fifty trade where I spent half the week with Ares and half the week with Achilles, but Ares refused to let me out of his sight, especially with our new knowledge that Maurice was after me.

Ares, Achilles, and Koda sat around a table inside Achilles' chambers discussing what to do next. I'd been sitting idly by, letting them debate with each other, but I couldn't hold back anymore.

"There's only one clear choice, but we need Victor in order to do it."

"What choice would that be?" Victor asked from the doorway.

I stood up and smiled at the handsome vampire. "Victor. It's nice to see you."

Victor was wearing all black and looking as sleek as ever. His all black eyes no longer bothered me, but made me realize exactly how powerful he was. He looked me up and down and smiled. "You're even more beautiful than you were when I first met you. Gaining your Sidhe powers has done wonders for you."

He walked forward and hugged me, ignoring Ares' growl. I stood on tiptoe and kissed his cheek. "You're such a sweet talker. I just hope you're willing to help us."

Victor and I stared at each other for ten full minutes of silence as I played out my plan in my head to him. Victor's vampiric ability, unlike any other of his kind, was to be able to hear people's thoughts. Victor listened intently and then arched one of his elegant black eyebrows. "Have you discussed this with Ares?"

I rolled my eyes. "Of course not. I wanted to discuss it with you first."

Victor laughed. "You're getting to know him better. That's good." He looked at Achilles and his eyebrow rose again. "You bound her?"

I groaned. "How can everybody tell that?"

Victor waved his hand in the air between Achilles and me. "Anyone with slight magical abilities can see the silver rope dangling between you two."

"I can't," I said with a pout.

Victor patted my hand. "You will. You're still very young.

You have to remember, the rest of us have had hundreds of years to practice."

Ares cleared his throat. "Can we get back to the matter at hand?"

Victor laughed. "Yes, of course." He looked at me and sighed. "I fear Artemis is right. The only way to end the attacks on her and the craziness that is my father, is to fight him."

Ares jumped up and shook his head. "No! Absolutely not! I will not risk Artemis in a fight against Maurice and his flock."

"Excuse me," said an incredibly deep French accented voice.

Ares looked towards the doorway and then grabbed me in his arms while growling loudly and baring his teeth at the newcomer.

The man was obviously a vampire, sleek built yet omitting loads of evil. He should have had a sign above his head that read, "badass".

He smiled and spoke softly, "I did not mean to upset you, *Groll.*"

Ares snarled. "State your intentions."

The man bowed. "I have come at Prince Victor's request."

Ares looked at Victor, his eyes narrowed. "You brought, *Fear?* You brought your father's number one assassin into the presence of my mate?"

Victor held up his hand, and Ares stopped his rant, setting me down on my feet. Victor pointed at the man Ares referred to as Fear. "One, he is not my father's assassin anymore. I blood bound him to me. Two, I brought him to assist me. Three, we will need his expertise if we are to fight my father's newest vampires. Four, I like him. He plays chess better than you and never turns me down when I ask for a match."

I raised my hand and everyone looked at me. I held up one finger. "One, why did you call him '*Groll*'?" I held up a second finger. "Two, why did you call him 'Fear'?"

Koda spoke from just behind me, having apparently moved forward when Ares growled, "He is referred to as 'Fear' because that's the last thing you feel before he kills you. You don't have a chance to look behind you or even to think someone might be behind you. All you know is that you feel fearful and then boom, you're dead."

Fear spoke then to me, "*Groll* literally means anger. Ares was the embodiment of *Groll* for centuries."

Ares had relaxed by then and linked his fingers with mine. "You will find that I no longer hold that title."

Fear laughed. "Oh, I think you do. Perhaps you are no longer *Groll* all the time as you once were, but he lives within you. Given the right circumstances, I believe *Groll* may resurrect himself. I believe when you fight to protect your mate you are not as calm as one should be."

Ares growled. "Careful, Fear."

The vampire bowed gracefully. "I meant no disrespect or threat."

"What's your real name?" I asked Fear.

He smiled and it made my heart beat faster in alarm. "You need not be frightened of me. I will not harm you. My name is Dmitri." He was suddenly in front of me and kissing the back of my hand. He inhaled loudly and smiled. "You smell good."

Ares growled. "Step back from my mate."

Dmitri winked at me and then was back by the door.

How did he move so fast? I couldn't even see a blurred trail of him. No wonder he was an assassin.

Victor, who had been standing idly by, now began speaking, "We need to go to my father and speak to him and if he won't listen to reason, attack him. He won't expect us to come there."

"He won't expect us to come there because it's a suicide mission!" Ares yelled as he started pacing around the room with his arms at his sides and his hands clenching and relaxing with each step.

Victor scoffed. "You have two of the most powerful vampires, the second in line of the Sidhe and Artemis at your side and you believe we cannot defeat an army of vampires and the King? You have no faith in us."

Ares rolled his eyes. "We have five, I will not count Artemis because I don't want her to fight. So, five of us against two hundred or more vampires, some of them three hundred years old, and you think we can win?"

Victor smiled with a gleam in his solid black eyes. "Yes."

Ares sighed. "I hate when you have that look. It means you have a plan that will involve me almost dying."

Victor groaned. "That was only once."

Ares said, "No, it was twice! The first time was when we battled the dragons. The second time was when we battled Genghis Khan."

Victor rubbed his temples. "The dragon incident was my fault, but you're the one who felt insulted by Genghis Khan. I didn't want to start a war with him."

Ares folded his arms over his chest. "You called his mother a whore."

Victor spread his arms out in emphasis. "She was! She took money from men in exchange for—"

"Dragons are real?" I asked loudly to sidetrack them.

Ares smiled. "They were real."

My mouth gaped. "You killed all the dragons?"

Victor said, "It wasn't our fault really. The dragons

wouldn't stop attacking us and before we knew it, we'd kill all of them."

"What about their eggs?" I asked.

Ares and Victor looked at each other a moment before looking back at me. "What do you mean?" Ares asked.

I laughed. "You're kidding, right?" Both men just stared at me. "Dragons are born from eggs, like birds, right?" Both men nodded. "So, if you killed all of the living dragons that still leaves behind whatever eggs they had laid."

Victor laughed. "Well that explains the dragon sightings a few years ago."

Ares shook his head. "Why didn't we think about the eggs?"

Victor shrugged. "Perhaps because we were both trying not to bleed to death from the various wounds we had. It was a long, delirious trip back down that mountain."

Achilles raised his hand and everyone turned to him. "I could bring a few additional Sidhe with us."

Ares growled. "No."

"You would rather risk Artemis' life than have a few extra Sidhe around you?" Achilles asked angrily.

Ares' jaw clenched tightly for a few moments before he spoke. "I would rather not have to owe you any favors."

Achilles muttered under his breath and then said, "What if we agree that it's mutually beneficial for us to assist you and agree that you owe us nothing?"

Ares growled, and I ran my hand down his forearm. "It would help if we had some extra magic. Especially since fire is a big weakness for vampires."

Ares sighed and wrapped his arms around me. "I hate it when you're right."

I laughed. "No, you just hate it when you're wrong."

~

IT TOOK them two days to agree upon the Sidhe we would be bringing and then an additional day to agree on the plan. Each day of sitting made my irritation grow and with it, the need to kill something. It horrified me how easy it was for me to kill now. It was as if once you killed someone, the next ones were nothing since you'd already broken the barrier. I wanted to believe that things could be accomplished by simple discussions, but after living in this world for only a few weeks I realized that killing was the only way to solve anything with them.

My attraction to Achilles continued to grow and soon I found I needed his touch almost as much as I needed Ares'. Ares explained that my attraction and the need for touch were side effects from being bound to Achilles.

Every day we were in the Light Court, I practiced my magic. With Erebus' help I was able to summon fire as easily as twitching my finger. He also helped me learn how to fly and how to use my wings properly. Koda and Dmitri helped me with my fighting skills at other times. By the fourth day when we were preparing to depart, I felt as though I could take on the entire vampire army on my own.

Ares prepared a bag for me with some of the dresses and things from the dresser in Achilles' room. I sat on the bed behind him as he packed. "So, we're going to walk in the front door of the vampire estate and just ask to speak to Maurice?"

Ares stuffed a few pairs of socks into the duffel bag. "Yep."

"Are you scared?" I asked him.

He stopped packing and turned around to face me. "I'm only worried about you. Victor is right that Maurice will not stop hunting you. I won't let him have you."

I smiled. "I know that you'll protect me as best as you can. I'm not asking that. I'm asking what you feel as you prepare for a battle?"

Ares shrugged. "I've gone into thousands of battles. Two-thirds of those battles, I wasn't expected to win and I did. I guess it's like stage fright. After the first few times you get over the fear and just accept that you have to do it."

Ares and I were alone in the bedroom since everyone else was off preparing for the battle. I hopped down off the bed and ran my fingertip down his chest. "This could be our last night together," I whispered.

Ares tilted my chin up and looked in my eyes. "This will not be our last night together. I will not lose you." He kissed me with the same passion with which he spoke to me. It made my toes curl and my head spin. He picked me up and laid me down gently on the bed, as he began untying the dress and corset. He was being gentle when I knew he was holding himself back, the need to mate was driving us both crazy. With both hands I grabbed the collar of his shirt and ripped it in half, exposing his upper body. He had a truly splendid body. I ran my hands along his muscles and then kissed his upper chest. Ares moaned and then ripped my dress and corset in half, exposing me. It took me less than ten seconds to tear at his pants, but it was worth it. The first time I'd ever seen him naked I hadn't truly appreciated his glory. Now, I sat back and took in every inch of him, starting from the top of his head and ending at his knees.

"I love you, Ares," I whispered before I kissed his lips.

He pulled back from our kiss and smiled, giving me one of the most beautiful true smiles, and whispered, "I love you, too."

∿

ARES and I walked hand-in-hand through the castle courtyard out to where everyone was gathered to step through the portal back into the human world. Various Sidhe watched us walk by, some with glares, while others had more curious expressions. Erebus, Eros, and Heracles, or as the Western States called him, Hercules, were the three Sidhe chosen to go with us.

Achilles kept his back to us as we walked up and instead of speaking to us, he simply opened the portal and stepped through, holding the door open for Erebus who was behind him. I could tell he was upset, but I couldn't figure out why.

Athena ran forward and hugged me tightly. "Stay safe, Daughter."

I kissed her cheek. "I am well protected, so do not worry."

She looked at Ares and sighed. "As much as I dislike this, I must admit that you are a different man with her. If she weren't so happy, I would press the issue." She stopped talking and looked at the ground before looking back up, a fierce expression on her face. "Keep her safe or you'll have to answer to me." She kissed my cheek and then walked away.

Everyone filed through the portal single file. Once inside, the portal closed and darkness surrounded us. Koda, Ares, and I growled softly and whined as we walked through the confined space. It still amazed me how a portal between dimensions felt like a stone staircase.

Achilles opened the other end of the portal and stepped out into sun. Everyone hurried out. I basked in the light for a moment and then approached Achilles. "Hey."

Achilles turned away from me and pointed behind us, where a forest started. "This is the way to go."

He started to walk away, and I grabbed his arm. "Achilles."

He sighed. "Yes, Artemis."

I moved to stand in front of him. "Why are you refusing to look at me? You're acting like I did something wrong?"

Ares grabbed my other hand and started to pull me away. "It's alright. He just needs a few moments alone," he said softly.

I growled. "Dammit. Stop acting like a sulking teenage boy! Talk to me."

Ares released my hand, and Achilles looked down at me. "I'm trying not to be mad at you because I understand that you don't know how this bond works, but my emotions are on edge on the moment."

"Explain," I said softly.

He sighed and rubbed his temples. "Through the bond, it lets me feel what you are feeling. I can't read your thoughts, though we can communicate telepathically when you don't have a wall up. For some reason, you're blocking me out so you don't feel anything I feel, which is why you don't understand…" He stopped talking and looked up at the sun.

"Don't understand what?" I asked.

"I can feel your emotions, such as love, lust and…euphoria," he said through gritted teeth.

I blushed and stepped back from him with my eyes on the ground. "Oh." He'd felt my emotions while Ares and I mated. I hadn't even considered that. I hadn't even thought about Achilles at the time. "I'm sorry."

Victor cleared his throat. "We should keep moving."

Everyone started walking away, but I stayed still, wanting a moment alone with Achilles. Ares seemed to understand and followed Koda who was walking behind Victor.

I looked up at Achilles. "I'm sorry. I didn't know. You

should have told me this before. I hate that you guys keep so much from me and then just let me stumble upon it like this. I really am sorry. I didn't mean to hurt you."

He smiled at me. "Thank you. All I wanted was a sincere apology." He pushed back a strand of my hair and whispered, "I love you, Artemis, which makes it incredibly difficult to stay mad at you."

I blinked at him. "You love me? Or do you mean you love me because of the bond thing?"

He shook his head and whispered, "I've loved you since you were born. Every summer I would sneak near your house to watch you grow up. Since the time you were sixteen, I could see how beautiful you were going to be. Now that I can see you since you've gained your Sidhe powers and can witness how great a woman you are, I love you even more."

I swallowed nervously. "Achilles—"

He put his fingertip to my mouth. "I know that you do not love me yet. I just hope that soon you will see that I love you as much as Ares does. Perhaps we can figure out a way for you to be happy with both of us. Whatever happens, it will not change the fact that for me, you're the only woman I want to be with. *Verus amor vincit omnia.* True love conquers all."

Before I could respond, he kissed me on the lips. The kiss started off gentle and then became more passionate. He caressed my back softly, and I lost myself in his touch. The barrier he'd been talking about in my head broke and images of him watching me as I grew up and then his current feelings bombarded me. He truly did love me and I knew he would do anything to keep me near him.

We broke apart and I gasped for air as I returned to my own thoughts. Achilles took my hand gently. "We should catch up with the others."

I realized his body and eyes were glowing and giggled. "Oops. Looks like I activated your powers again."

He sighed. "Yes, so it seems."

We started walking and Victor called from within the trees. "Could you turn off the light? You look like a damn Glowworm doll."

I giggled and then focused on my Sidhe powers and the connection I could now feel between Achilles and me. I poked him in the arm and said, "Off." His body returned to normal. I poke him again and said, "On," and he began glowing again.

Achilles smacked my hand as I reached towards him again. "That's enough. No more Glowworm jokes."

We caught up to the others, who had waited for us in a clearing, and I hurried to walk between Ares and Achilles.

Ares asked, "Aren't Glowworm's supposed to sing when you turn them on?"

I giggled. "No, they just play music."

Achilles snapped his fingers. "Darn. I forgot my flute."

Erebus said, "I just happen to have..."

Achilles sighed. "*Enough* with the Glowworm references."

We continued walking for three hours and then we came to the ocean. I frowned as I looked up and down the beach for a boat. "Um, how are we going to cross this?"

Dmitri's and Victor's bodies convulsed and shrunk as they changed shapes to two black bats. Vampires could turn into shadow, mist, wolves, *and* bats. I really needed a notebook to keep track of it all.

Erebus, Eros, Achilles, and Heracles let their wings out and I smiled. "Oh, I see." I was very glad that I'd put on a top with a low back as I let my wings out. I was glad I had practiced.

Ares and Koda stood in front of Erebus and Achilles, who picked them up, and then everyone was airborne. I flew after them and then followed the two black bats as they led the way to France. I trailed my hand in the ocean for a little bit and then flew up as high as I could, reaching for the moon before coming back down and joining the others. "I love flying," I said wistfully.

Erebus smiled and spoke in his incredibly deep voice, "The nighttime is the best for flying."

It only took us one hour to fly from Ireland to France, but I was tired by the time we arrived. We made camp in a wooded area which was a short trip from the vampires' nest.

I found an area with few rocks and laid down in the dirt. Ares appeared next to me, but in wolf form. He was as handsome in his wolf form as he was as a man. I ran my hands through his thick black fur and kissed the tip of his large nose. As far as I had seen, Ares was the only black werewolf. It made me wonder why. I'd also never seen another white werewolf like me. Was it because of our mixed genetics? Ares laid down in the dirt, and I scooted closer to him, letting his large wolf body circle around mine.

Koda approached us, also in wolf form and lay down facing Ares. He extended his paws so that they overlapped Ares'. Taking the hint, I laid my head on top of their front paws and let them arrange themselves comfortably.

The sun rose earlier than I would have liked the next morning. I started to stretch when I remembered the vampires. I bolted upright, knocking Ares' and Koda's heads to the sides as I searched for them.

Victor smiled at me, and I remembered he was a born vampire and the sun didn't harm him. "Your concern brings a smile to my face, *mon papillon*. Dmitri is safely buried so you need not worry for him," he said softly.

I exhaled and calmed my raging heart. "Sorry." I laid back

down against Ares and he sighed, rearranging himself around me. I slept for a couple more hours and then my stomach grumbled incessantly.

Ares headed into the trees and came out a few moments later dressed in blue jeans and a t-shirt.

Koda was whining and kicking his hind leg as Ares walked back, but after a quick throat clearing from Ares, Koda was awake and groaning unhappily as he trotted towards the trees.

Ares wrapped his arms around me and asked, "So, what's for breakfast?"

Victor straightened his shirt and said, "I thought it would be nice if we took Artemis out."

I looked over at the black, white, and red Sidhe men, all with various vine and etched designs in their skin, sitting a few yards away. "Don't you think the designs on our skin might draw attention to us?"

The Sidhe men laughed and all stood up. Their bodies began to glow softly and then each of them had normal looking skin. They looked as though they belonged in Greece.

Achilles smiled. "We learned how to use glamour when we were going to be around the humans."

"Glamour?" I asked.

Erebus said, "It's a specific type of magic which alters our physical appearance."

"Oh. Well how do I do it?" I asked.

Achilles picked my hands up and whispered, "Close your eyes. Picture what you looked like before you came into your Sidhe powers, and pull at your powers."

I did as he said and when I opened my eyes, I couldn't believe that it had actually worked.

Victor stood and dusted his jeans. "Are we all ready?"

Koda came out of the woods in jeans and a t-shirt and nodded. "Yeah, let's go."

Victor led the way to a small café where we could sit outside in the warm sunlight. Ares ordered my food for me since I couldn't read the menu which was in French. It was nice having someone who could speak multiple languages so I didn't look like a dumb American traveler.

Our food came out quickly, and I ate every last bite. I hadn't realized how hungry I was, and I was thankful that Ares had ordered extra sides of eggs and bacon for me.

The men started talking in French, and I felt extremely left out.

Achilles smiled at me from across the table and then began talking to me telepathically. *They're discussing the best place to have the Sidhe wait. I will be going with you into the main door, but the other three will wait outside for our signal.*

What signal?

Oh you'll know it when you see it.

As the morning turned into afternoon, the men continued to plan and Achilles continued to translate for me. The plan was rather simple, but they were being very meticulous about the small details. We ordered lunch at the same café and sipped on wine until dinner time. I was feeling pretty light-headed when dinner came, but my quick metabolism flushed out the alcohol the third time I used the restroom. Each time I went to the restroom, one of the men would accompany me, though each time it was a different man. After we finished our dinner, we walked back to the park and sat down in our camp spot.

As soon as the sun went down an arm shot out of the dirt in front of me, making me gasp and jump backwards.

Victor patted my arm and pulled me back down on the ground beside him. "It's just Dmitri, rising for the night."

Dmitri dug himself out of the ground and then shook like a dog to get the excess dirt off of him. Victor stood, and together they left to hunt for their meals.

I picked up a leaf and set it in the palm of my hand and then brought fire to my hand, burning the green leaf. I formed a ball of fire in one palm and then started tossing the ball back and forth in my hands.

Erebus watched me with a small smile of satisfaction on his face.

"Catch," I yelled as I tossed the purple ball at him. Erebus caught the ball of fire and it changed to a black ball of fire. He started playing with it before he tossed it to Achilles who changed it to a blue flame, played with it for a while and then tossed it back to me. As soon as I touched it, the flames turned purple.

"Why does the color change?" I asked.

Erebus said, "The flame changes to match our colors. So anytime you use fire or touch it, it will become purple while Achilles will always turn it blue. We aren't quite sure why it happens, but it does."

We occupied ourselves with that for the next thirty minutes while we waited for Victor and Dmitri. They returned and stood twenty yards away from us as they watched our game.

"Could you please put that out?" Dmitri asked.

Achilles tossed the ball up in the air. It went up and up and then disappeared completely.

Dmitri smiled. "Thank you."

Victor looked at Ares and smiled. "It's time."

Ares exhaled. "Alright. Let's go."

We ran for an hour through the city streets, just fast enough the humans wouldn't see us as we ran. As we approached the mansion, I could feel the evil that resided there—the hundreds of vampires and the king of evil himself, Maurice.

My heartbeat picked up and my palms began to sweat. What if we couldn't defeat him? What if Ares died? The thought of Ares dying ripped at my heart and brought tears to my eyes.

I couldn't let him die. I had to keep him safe.

Victor guided us through a back entrance and then we were at the front doors. The guards opened the doors and bowed as we walked by. Victor led the way through the giant mansion and into a large ballroom. Crystal chandeliers hung from the ceilings and made me feel as though we'd been taken back to another time period.

"Greetings," Maurice said. His voice sent shivers down my spine and would have made me tuck my tail between my legs if I were in wolf form.

Ares picked my hand up gently, and his reassurance gave me strength.

Victor walked forward and bowed. "Greetings, Father."

Maurice's gaze never left mine as we walked towards his throne. The throne seemed to be carved out of a single, giant piece of gold and glittered with gems. "I'm so happy that you came."

"Father, we have heard a rumor that the vampires and dhampirs that have been hounding Artemis may have been sent by you. Is this true?" Victor spoke in such a calm voice that I almost believed he was simply asking about a rumor.

Maurice began speaking, but I realized he was speaking to me. "I can give you anything in the world that you want. I could let you rule an entire nation if you wanted. Whatever you want, tell me and it'll be yours if you join me."

"I can't join you. I can't allow you to kill off the entire human race." I frowned.

Maurice stood up. "Join me, or those you love die!"

I looked at Ares and then at Achilles who were both smiling at me. It was then that I realized no matter how much I wanted to keep Ares and Achilles safe, they would have to fight beside me to accomplish our safety. I squeezed Ares' hand and looked back up at Maurice. "*Verus amor vincit omnia.* True love conquers all. No, I will not join you. I will not leave the ones I love. I will stand beside them and fight you, and die if I have to."

Maurice's face changed, and I saw his true face, his vampire face, and immediately my skin went cold. The King of Vampires in battle mode was something no human should witness. He was truly frightening.

The doors to the ballroom started to shake and Victor yelled, "Get ready!"

Achilles' body burst into bright color and he raised his hand straight up over his head, shooting a blue fireball through the ceiling.

That must be the signal.

Achilles smiled at me and then Erebus, Eros, and Heracles flew in through the ceiling. As soon as they landed, the fight began.

Hundreds of vampires poured in through the ballroom doors and headed towards us. Ares body rippled as he took a half-shift and started attacking the vampires with Koda beside him in wolf form.

Achilles shot fireball after fireball at the vampires, catching some on fire and tearing holes through others.

Victor and Dmitri pulled out swords as they fought against their own kind.

Erebus, Eros, and Heracles fought in a small circle with their backs together.

I stood in the center of them all and smiled. It was my turn to fight. It was my turn to prove my worth.

Closing my eyes, I concentrated on the powers that resided within me, and focused on the plants outside of the building and all of the living things nearby to draw on their power. I summoned a portion of my energy, turned my hands into paws with extended claws and opened my eyes. My body was glowing brighter than anyone else's, making the vampires shield their eyes. I screamed my battle cry and leaped into the battle. Bodies fell before my wrath as my primal fighting instincts took over.

I thought we were winning, but as soon as we killed a portion of the vampires in the room, more would come in to replace them. I started moving further away from my group when I saw him…my dad.

Darren stood beside Maurice and was looking out over the battle. His eyes stopped on me and he growled, his lip pulling up in a snarl. He moved away from Maurice and towards me.

I tried to head back towards Achilles and Ares, but the vampires had clustered together to keep us separated. I couldn't fight Darren. I couldn't win against him.

"Ares!" I yelled frantically as Darren came closer to me.

Ares stopped his fighting and turned towards me, his eyes widening when he saw Darren. Ares started to make his way, but he was too far and there were too many vampires blocking him. I turned around in search of Achilles, but I couldn't see him over the vampires standing in front of me. I clawed and slashed and burned the vampires, but no matter how many I killed I couldn't get closer to Ares or farther from Darren.

Suddenly Darren's hand grabbed me by the hair and jerked me backwards. I yelled in surprise and he put his hand around my throat. "I should have done this eighteen years ago."

I struggled against him. "Please, Dad. Please."

Darren smiled. "Did you actually think I loved you? Did you think I could love a halfbreed? You were nothing more than a mistake. I wanted to mate with your mother, but I didn't want you. I never wanted you."

His words hurt worse than anything I could have imagined. "Then why did you raise me? Why keep me alive?" I asked as tears leaked down my face.

"I was training you for Maurice, but then you had to go and betray me by leaving with Ares."

"I didn't betray you. He's my destined mate. Please dad. Don't do this."

Darren laughed. "You're pathetic." His hand tightened around my throat and my air cut off. I gasped for air and clawed at Darren, but no matter how many gashes I opened, his grip didn't loosen. Spots crowded my vision as I began to go unconscious. Ares yelled, and then I was on the floor, gasping for air. I turned around and watched as Darren and Ares fought. I'd never thought of Darren as terrifying, but as I watched him fight Ares, he was one of the most terrifying beings on the planet.

Darren changed into his wolf form and jumped a few yards away for a chance to recover. Ares changed forms as well and charged after Darren. I wanted to keep watching, to help if I could, but the vampires surrounding me had started moving closer. Achilles yelled in pain at the same instant that Ares did.

Maurice yelled, "Join me, Artemis, and this can all end!"

White hot anger flowed through my veins. Death. I wanted all of these vampires dead. Permanently dead. I wanted my loved ones free. I wanted to be free. I closed my eyes and prayed to whoever or whatever might be listening to help me. I had to save them. Warm wind surrounded me in a mini tornado and then power filled me. I'd never felt so much power before and it made me dizzy. I stood up and whispered, "Kill the vampires." I felt as though my skin was going to burst and then all of the power left me in a giant explosion. I screamed as the rush of power left me and fell to the ground on my hands and knees.

The room was eerily silent as I opened my eyes and stood up. I soon realized why. Every vampire, except Maurice, Dmitri and Victor were gone. Ash sifted through the air, but no bodies remained.

Maurice yelled, "Now!"

I looked for Ares, but couldn't see him. I tried to stand, but strong hands grabbed me.

Ares and Achilles screamed, "No!" in unison and then I was traveling through a black spinning vortex I recognized too well. The spinning stopped and my nausea quickly vanished. I gaped at the house Darren had raised me in.

I spun around and glared at Hera. "What are you doing?"

Her body glowed and she never looked so much like a goddess as she did then. She placed her hands on each side of my head and whispered, "What is necessary for my son's survival." She started speaking in another language and then pain filled every cell of my body.

I started to scream, but horror froze my limbs as I realized what she was doing. She was stealing my memories. The fight with Maurice. The last night that Ares and I made love.

Achilles telling me he loved me. The training with the Sidhe. Matt's death. Victor. Matt. Koda. Achilles. Ares. I screamed and fought against her, but she was too strong, and I was too weak.

Every memory that I cherished was pulled from me and increased the hole I felt widening inside of my heart. People's faces whom I loved began to disappear. I couldn't remember my mother. I couldn't remember what Koda or Achilles looked like. I couldn't remember Ares scent or his face.

"Ares!" I screamed as the memories of him disappeared in a flash of painful magic.

Hera screamed and then released me as I fainted.

TEN

The woman standing before me was stunning. She was glowing as though an internal light was on. Part of me wanted to call it her powers, but I didn't understand what it meant.

She smiled down at me and held out her hand to help me stand up. "Are you alright, child?"

I rubbed my sore head and stood up on shaky legs. "I...I think so." I looked around at the place I was in and asked, "Where am I?"

She whispered, "You're safe and so is everyone else. That's all that matters for now."

"What do you mean? Who are you?"

She shook her head. "I'm sorry, but I cannot tell you that."

In a flash of light, she disappeared and I was alone. Had she been a goddess? Or perhaps a witch?

I rubbed my hands down my arms, realized I was naked, but decided it wasn't important at the moment, and turned to look at everything around me. I was in front of a house, but it didn't seem particularly special to me. A town was near, I could smell gasoline from vehicles, but I couldn't smell people. That seemed odd, but I didn't let it bother me at the moment.

I smelled trees nearby and that drew my attention. I stepped into the shelter of the trees and heard a wolf howl in the distance.

A wolf. Yes, I was part wolf. A…a werewolf. I could switch forms if I wanted to.

I closed my eyes and willed the wolf side of me to take over. My body changed and I ran deeper into the forest, calling out to any of my brothers or sisters that might be nearby. I felt lonely. So incredibly lonely that it hurt. Not just emotionally, but physically as well.

A pack of small wolves came from the shadows of the forest and surrounded me. These were obviously not were-wolves like me, for one they were much smaller and didn't exude the same presence werewolves should, but I needed a pack to run with. I couldn't stand this loneliness anymore. I wouldn't survive this loneliness.

I dropped my head submissively and whined, asking to join their pack. The alpha, a grey wolf with a large scar down his throat, walked forward and growled at me. I dropped to the ground, and he moved forward to sniff my stomach. The rest of the pack came forward and I was recognized as a friend. The pack ran and I ran with it, now a member of it.

That was strange, too. Why would the pack accept me so quickly? So many strange things without answers. So many questions. So many unknowns.

There was something important I was supposed to be doing, but I couldn't remember what. I felt something missing inside me. Two big things. Yes, there were two things missing inside of me, as though pieces of my heart were gone, but I couldn't remember what to do to make me whole again. I didn't even remember what had happened to cause the emptiness.

I shook my head, cleared the human thoughts, and let the animal within me take over. I barked and ran after the others, happy in the moment of the chase as we raced after a herd of deer.

THE STORY CONTINUES...

To find out what happens next, check out Healed by the Fire, the next book in the Artemis Lupine Series.

CONNECT WITH CATHERINE BANKS

I really appreciate you reading my book! I hope you enjoyed it.

Please consider leaving a review at your favorite site.

Here are some ways to connect with me:

www.catherinebanks.com

Follow me on BookBub: https://www.bookbub.com/authors/catherine-banks

Join my Patreon: http://www.patreon.com/catherinebanks

Purchase items handmade by Catherine: http://Etsy.com/shop/TurboKittenInd

About the Author

Catherine Banks is a USA Today bestselling fantasy author who writes in several fantasy subgenres and has multiple pseudonyms. She began writing fiction at only four years old and finished her first full-length novel at the age of fifteen. She is married to her soulmate and best friend, Avery, who she has two amazing children with. After her full-time job, she reads books, plays video games, and watches anime shows and movies with her family to relax. Although she has lived in Northern California her entire life, she dreams of traveling around the world. Catherine is also C.E.O. of Turbo Kitten Industries™, a company with many hats including being a book publisher and Etsy store full of nerdy fun.

facebook.com/catherinebanksauthor
twitter.com/catherineebanks
amazon.com/author/catherinebanks
bookbub.com/authors/catherine-banks

MORE FROM CATHERINE BANKS

ADULT PARANORMAL & FANTASY ROMANCE SERIES

Zodiac Shifters Paranormal Romance Series

Centaur's Prize

Tiger Tears

Lion About

Ciara Steele Novella Series

True Faces

Barbaric Tendencies

ADULT REVERSE HAREM PARANORMAL & FANTASY ROMANCE SERIES

Her Royal Harem Series

Royally Entangled

Royally Exposed

Royally Elected

Royally Enraged

Her Royal Harem, The Complete Series

The Demon's Fair

Her Royal Harem, The Coloring Book

Wings of Vengeance Series

Of Dragons and Cruelty

Of Minotaurs and Sacrifice

Wings of Vengeance, The Complete Series

Anderelle: Minloa Trilogy

Queen of the Stars

Empress of the Galaxy

Goddess of the Universe

Anderelle: Minloa, The Complete Series

Bonds of Madness Series
Sealing the Deal
Racing the Clock

Her Super Harem Series
Lucky Strike

Her Hellish Harem Duet
A Demon's Heart
A Demon's Soul*

*Coming Soon

MORE FROM CATHERINE BANKS

STANDALONE YOUNG ADULT PARANORMAL & FANTASY ROMANCE BOOKS

Monster Academy

Daughter of Lions

Lady Serra and the Draconian

Of Sky and Sea

The Last Werewolf

Sybil Deceived

STANDALONE YOUNG ADULT PARANORMAL & FANTASY REVERSE HAREM ROMANCE BOOKS

Moon Academy

STANDALONE ADULT PARANORMAL & FANTASY ROMANCE BOOKS

Demonic Contract

Anja's Secret

Dragon's Blood

Last Ama Princess

Transforming Rose
Alys of Asgard
Phoenix Possessed
Stone Heart

STANDALONE URBAN FANTASY BOOKS
The Pawn

CHILDREN'S BOOKS
Calvin's Alien Adventure

MORE FROM DAISY EMORY

The Boyfriend Deal

Their Purple Girl

ACCIDENTAL MOBSTER SERIES
Accidental Mobster
Unintentional Pirate
Suddenly Baroness*

*Coming Soon